"It's t[...] *on yourself."*

Matt's voice was gentle as he spoke to Margaret. "Tim can take care of himself. He's able to make the right decisions."

"I did not come here for a lecture on my life-style," she said furiously.

"Don't make Tim your excuse for avoiding life, Margaret," Matt continued, as if she hadn't spoken. "There's more to living than watching out for your brother."

Margaret glared at him as the last vestige of her self-control shattered.

"I know exactly what's behind all this." Her voice was low and strained. "You can't believe my refusal to join the Matthew Magnum fan club. Well, let me tell you, Mr. Magnum, that no matter how long you stay in town, my attitude toward you isn't going to change."

Matt held her gaze steadily. "Is that what you really think, Margaret? That my main purpose in staying here is to *seduce* you into seeing things my way?"

Dear Reader,

What a fabulous lineup we have this month at Silhouette Romance. We've got so many treats in store for you that it's hard to know where to begin! Let's start with our WRITTEN IN THE STARS selection. Each month in 1992, we're proud to present a Silhouette Romance novel that focuses on the hero and his astrological sign. This month we're featuring the charming, handsome Libra man in Tracy Sinclair's *Anything But Marriage*.

Making his appearance this month is another one of our FABULOUS FATHERS. This delightful new series celebrates the hero as father, and the hero of Toni Collins's *Letters from Home* is a very special father, indeed.

To round out the month, we have warm, wonderful love stories from Pepper Adams, Geeta Kingsley, Vivian Leiber, and as an added treat, we have Silhouette Romance's first PREMIERE author, Patricia Thayer. PREMIERE is a Silhouette special event to showcase bright, new talent.

In the months to come, watch for Silhouette Romance novels by many more of your favorite authors, including Diana Palmer, Annette Broadrick and Marie Ferrarella.

The Silhouette Romance authors and editors love to hear from readers, and we'd especially love to hear from *you*.

Happy reading from all of us at Silhouette!

Valerie Susan Hayward
Senior Editor

TENDER TRUCKER
Geeta Kingsley

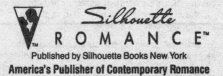

Silhouette
R O M A N C E™
Published by Silhouette Books New York
America's Publisher of Contemporary Romance

For my son—you've made my life richer.

SILHOUETTE BOOKS
300 E. 42nd St., New York, N.Y. 10017

TENDER TRUCKER

Copyright © 1992 by Geeta M. Kakade

ISBN: 0-373-08894-9

First Silhouette Books printing October 1992

Books by Geeta Kingsley

Silhouette Romance

Faith, Hope and Love #726
Project Valentine #775
Tender Trucker #894

GEETA KINGSLEY

is a former elementary school teacher who loves traveling, music, needlework and gardening. Raised in an army family, she was never lonely as long as she had books to read. She now lives in Southern California with her husband, two teenagers and the family dog. Her first published novel, *Faith, Hope and Love,* was a finalist in the Romance Writers of America's RITA competition.

Geeta believes in the triumph of the human spirit and this, along with her concern for the environment, is reflected in her characters and stories.

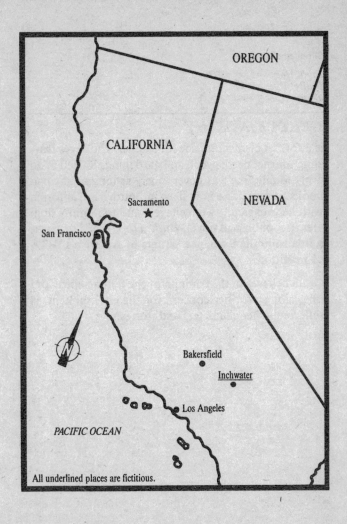

OREGON

CALIFORNIA

NEVADA

Sacramento ★

San Francisco

Bakersfield

Inchwater

Los Angeles

PACIFIC OCEAN

N

All underlined places are fictitious.

Chapter One

The blue letters on a white background signified her worst nightmare come true. Margaret Browning stared at the sign for a full minute. Bedouin Trucking. Higher up, on a huge pole so it was visible from the freeway, was another sign. Truck Stop, it proclaimed to everyone around.

Margaret closed her eyes and wished it all away. Opening them a second later she found everything still there. She turned her gaze to the enormous brick and glass structure that had replaced Simm's old dilapidated garage. The modern truck stop looked out of place in Inchwater, California, where the term *new* was applied to things ten years old, and the outside of every building had durable, practical, aluminum siding.

"Why here?" She wasn't aware of saying the words aloud.

"Why not?" her companion in the battered sedan answered. "Magnum said he needed to expand. Land in Los Angeles costs the earth. Besides, he wanted a place somewhere between L.A. and Las Vegas, on the routes his drivers use most frequently. He picked Inchwater for all the above reasons, plus the fact no one objected to having it here.''

No one except herself, and she hadn't been here to voice a protest. The thought of her brother having anything to do with the truck stop frightened her.

"I wonder what Timmy's doing here?" she asked, almost to herself.

Margaret turned to Joe Graines. Her high school classmate had picked her up at the nearest airport to Inchwater—over seventy miles away. Busy fiddling with the car radio, he seemed not to have heard her question.

Anxious to see her brother, Margaret had asked Joe to stop off at Dan's Donuts before heading to the diner. Timmy had been working at Dan's since January. To her surprise Dan had told her she would find Timmy at the truck stop.

Well, she was here now, and there was no sign of Timmy, which meant she would have to go in and ask for him.

"Thanks for the ride, Joe." Margaret smiled.

"Sure you don't want me to stick around and drive you home?" Joe Graines asked amiably.

"No, I need the walk." She also needed time alone to sort through the jumble of her thoughts.

"See you later, then," Joe said as Margaret got out of the car. "I'll drop your luggage off at Janet's."

"Later," Margaret echoed, her mind occupied with her surroundings. "And thanks again for meeting my plane."

"Bye Margaret."

It was her father who had insisted everybody call her Margaret. Not Marge, or Peggy or even Meg. Simply Margaret. It was the name of a princess, he'd always maintained, and shortening it would ruin it.

As the car roared off, Margaret took a deep breath and turned toward the truck stop. Being here reminded her of her father and the work he had done. Trucking had killed both her parents, snatching them from her and Timmy.

As truck stops went, this was one of the best she had ever seen. The hundred feet of dirt that had separated Simm's garage from the main road was paved now, the asphalt hard under her shoes. There were trucks all around of every shape and size. Neatly parked, being filled, being washed or simply standing there. Most of them were blue and silver and had a silver unicorn emblazoned on the side along with the words Bedouin Trucking. Diesel pumps lined one side of the yard. Fifty yards from the entrance stood a building marked Office. Glassed in on four sides, it allowed a clear view of all that went on in the truck stop. At the rear, the huge brick building she'd noticed earlier housed more trucks in various stages of repair.

Margaret headed for the office. Maybe someone there could tell her where Timmy was.

As she looked around, sensations swamped her, bringing her to a dead halt. Margaret took a deep breath. The atmosphere here had a strange effect on her. The shouts of the drivers calling to each other, the throb of the running engines, the smell of diesel and grease, the men and women milling about were all sparks lighting the dry heap of memories she'd locked away so carefully.

Pictures from the past danced out of the bonfire. Too hot. Too close.

Daddy.

It was the poignant cry of a child whom death had cheated of her parents' love.

Margaret raised a hand to her mouth to hold the cry back as another image surfaced.

"Look, Daddy, I can drive your truck."

It was one of her earliest memories; sitting on his lap, being allowed to turn the steering wheel of the parked rig. The texture of the sheepskin cover her mother had made for the wheel tickled her palms, making her giggle. The

smell had been the same. Diesel and grease. Then it had
been bearable, because the perfume her mother used had
been mixed with it. Now it simply whipped her memories
into a frenzy. Her father had dropped a kiss on top of her
head and said, "You make a mighty fine truck driver,
sweetheart."

A big, burly man turned and waved to someone in the
yard, and another picture jumped to the forefront. Daddy
had always turned to wave, just like that, before he
climbed into his truck.

*"Be a good girl for Aunt Janet, Margaret, and we'll
have a surprise for you when we get back."*

A couple stepped into the cab of their rig. To Margaret's tortured imagination, they were her parents getting
ready to leave on another trip.

"Mommy, Daddy, don't go away."

She had to stop them. This was the last trip; the one her
parents had never returned from. Margaret could taste the
disaster on her tongue. Bitter, awful, *searing.*

Matt watched the woman approach through the glass.
The flaming red hair made her look like a lit torch. The rest
of her was slim. Fashionably dressed in high heels and a
suit, she stood out like a sore thumb in the yard.

He frowned as he noticed the way she clutched her bag
in one white-knuckled hand. His eyes narrowed as she
came closer and he took in the stricken expression on her
face, the hand over her mouth. *What the hell?* Instinct had
him heading toward the door as she stepped off the concrete median.

"Look out!" The shout reached Margaret's ears at the
same time she felt herself being lifted in the air and put
down. The sound of a passing truck jolted her back to the
present, leaving her cold and shaky.

"Are you trying to get yourself killed?"

Large hands encircled her waist, as their owner waited for an answer.

"No." Margaret blinked rapidly, tilting her head back to get a look at the person who held her. The sun in her eyes made it impossible to make out anything, except that he was very big.

The hands at her waist were removed and Margaret turned around slowly to find her nose half an inch away from a button. A white button on a green-white-and-black checked shirt. Taking a cautious step back, she raised her gaze to a pair of eyes viewing her with undisguised hostility.

Margaret lifted her chin. Nice eyes, a part of her dazed brain registered. Forest green. Nice smell, too. Pine.

Nice stopped there, though. The rest was all angry man.

"What was that all about?" Her tone held one part bravado, two parts ice.

"Suppose you tell me?" His features looked as if they had been carved from rock. Her gaze fixed on the deep cleft in his chin. He sounded like the rain in a temper. Strong, powerful, *dangerous.* "One minute you're mincing along the concrete median, and the next you're stepping off it, directly into the path of a reversing truck."

"The driver has mirrors powerful enough to see a cockroach in his path," Margaret retorted, angered by his choice of words.

Mincing brought to mind an airhead in a too tight skirt, with fluff instead of a brain in her cerebral cavity. She resented the implication.

"Only a psychic could know you were going to stop staring at everything like a kid at the circus, and step off the median as if you're sleepwalking. What are you doing here, anyway? If you're collecting for a local charity, do us a favor and just write next time, okay?"

"There's no need to be rude," Margaret said stiffly.

"There is, if your jaywalking is going to endanger you and us. The name's Magnum. Matthew Magnum. Can I help you in any way?"

Margaret wet her dry lips. Joe had mentioned the name. She looked at the owner of Bedouin Trucking and tried to appear cool, calm and collected. As he surveyed her from head to toe, cool and calm disintegrated, and collected seemed like a lost cause. Margaret resisted the impulse to button the jacket of the navy suit she wore.

Magnum's gaze returned to her face, "The mall is in the opposite direction. This is a truck stop."

"I know where the mall is," Margaret snapped. "I'm looking for my brother, Timothy Browning. Is he here?"

Matthew Magnum's eyes narrowed, and he looked at her again, as if he were seeing her for the first time. Then he nodded to himself. "Thought the red hair and freckles looked familiar. The mouths are different, though."

She had to give him a ten for his powers of observation. Most people said except for their mouths, Timmy and she might have been twins.

"So you're the prodigal niece I've heard so much about?"

Margaret's mouth fell open. *Prodigal* niece?

"Home for the summer from D.C., are you?"

She nodded. He didn't seem to approve of her or her job in Washington. Confused, Margaret wondered what there was about teaching to arouse antagonism.

"It's about time you came home."

"Why?" asked Margaret.

His eyes narrowed. "Why? Just pull your head out of your private section of sand, and you'll see why. Your aunt has too much on her hands with the restaurant and your brother to care for, while you live it up." Before she could say a word, Matthew Magnum turned away. "Tim!"

The stentorian yell made her jump, and she glared at his broad back for a moment. She could no more live it up on her salary than the dodo could make a comeback. And why had he just implied she was an ostrich, oblivious to what went on around her? What was the man's middle name anyway? Grouch? He had to be the most abrasive person she had ever met.

Margaret's thoughts shifted as she saw her brother's lanky figure emerge from one of the enormous sheds at the rear. Tim had grown a couple of inches and seemed all hands and legs. Margaret smiled.

"Yes, Matt?"

Matthew Magnum jerked a thumb over his shoulder, and Timmy's eyes grew round when he saw her. A little of Margaret's pleasure evaporated as she realized Timmy's reaction to her presence held more shock than surprise.

"Take five," Matthew Magnum called over his shoulder as he entered the office, shutting the door behind him.

"Hello, Timmy." Margaret's raised arms fell to her sides as she realized her brother had no intention of being hugged. "How are you?"

"I'm fine, sis." Timmy rammed his hands into his pockets. "Did you have a good flight?"

Margaret nodded. The red-eye special from Washington had been nothing out of the ordinary.

"What did he mean, take five?"

The smell of diesel didn't bother her as much as the sullen look on her brother's face.

"Just that. I work here."

The world tilted to a forty-five degree angle and took its time straightening, as the last shreds of hope that Timmy was simply hanging out here were whipped away. "I thought you worked in Dan's Donuts?"

Her brother looked away. "I did, till I got this job. I like working around trucks better."

"I see."

True, their only contact in the last month had been brief telephone conversations, but Timmy could have told her about this new job.

If he'd wanted to.

Somewhere in the psychology classes she had taken in college, Margaret had learned not to make a fuss about things she didn't like. Angry reactions emphasized negative behavior, fixed it in the mind, put the person on the defensive. She took a deep breath. "I just stopped by Dan's, and he told me I'd find you here." It didn't seem worth it to tell Timmy she'd thought Dan had meant he had the day off and was simply hanging out at the truck stop with a friend.

Instead of replying, Timmy stared at a spot over her head.

"What time do you get through?"

That's the way, Margaret. Just play it nice and light.

"Five."

"Shall I pick you up, and we can go to a movie in Garrison?" They shared a passion for movies.

"Maybe another night. I'm going out with T.J. after work." Where the Timmy of yesterday would have smiled over mention of his girlfriend, the young adult of today refused to meet her gaze.

"That's great," Margaret said, as the hollow feeling inside increased. Timmy had never been distant with her before.

Everything that had happened in the last half hour seemed to assume gigantic proportions simply because she was tired, Margaret told herself. The man, Timmy's behavior, her own uneasiness, everything would sort itself out.

"I'll see you later, sis," Timmy said awkwardly. "My break's up."

"Later."

Margaret left the truck stop, keeping a lookout for the big rigs and angry men. On the main street, she turned left. Two hundred miles north of Los Angeles, Inchwater was little more than a rest area for travelers. Except for a couple of gas stations, three restaurants, a grocery store and a motel, the owners of which either lived above or behind their business, there was nothing else here. The nearest mall was nine miles away in Garrison. The resident population in Inchwater averaged fifteen because people preferred to live in Garrison and commute to Inchwater. The Inner Man, the restaurant her aunt owned, was only a couple of blocks away.

Margaret lifted her face into the air as she walked, picking up her stride, telling herself exercise was all she needed to blow the mental cobwebs away.

Timmy working around trucks didn't mean a thing. It was natural for him to prefer working there to frying doughnuts for Dan. It didn't indicate he was following in Daddy's footsteps.

Her pace slowed.

Their father had been a truck driver for twenty-four years when his truck had been found at the bottom of a small slope with both her parents dead inside.

Blocked arteries, the autopsy had revealed. It was the result of an unsettled life—too many beers, too many greasy hamburgers eaten at stop-and-go places because of delivery deadlines. Her father had suffered a heart attack that had caused him to lose control of his rig, the hospital authorities had informed Aunt Jan. It was nobody's fault.

But Margaret knew better. She knew it was the long hours, the kind of work he did that had caused her father's death.

It was ironic that Aunt Jan had decided to open The Inner Man, a restaurant for truckers. But The Inner Man was a fitting shrine to their parents, especially Daddy. Every single item on the menu was carefully selected to be low in

cholesterol, low in fat, and yet satisfying. Health awareness made The Inner Man a popular stop these days for
truckers and tourists.

Using the gate that led into the garden at the rear of the
restaurant, Margaret entered the kitchen.

Janet Hooper looked up from the whole wheat piecrust
she was rolling. A smile lit her face as she hurried around
the old, oak table to greet her niece. "Margaret! Welcome
home, darling!"

Home was Aunt Jan's arms around her, the warmth of
her presence, the love in her smile. They held each other
close, their gladness at being together transmitted without
words.

This kitchen had been the scene of so many homecom-
ings through the years. The aroma of baking bread clung
to the air, mixed with the scent of a roast in the oven. As
Aunt Jan hurried to fetch her a cup of coffee, Margaret
noticed the kitchen counters had been redone. Crisp new
curtains hung at the window that overlooked the garden,
and a row of shiny copper pans gleamed against the wall.
From outside the kitchen came the sound of voices in the
restaurant mixed with the clink of dishes being rinsed in
the work area beyond the kitchen. She had missed it all.

Margaret looked at Aunt Jan, immediately noticing the
new lines that creased her forehead, the tired look in her
eyes. Rake thin, immaculately turned out, it was hard for
strangers to imagine Janet Hooper's passion for cooking
and work. "How are you, Aunt Jan?"

"Never better," her aunt said briskly. "Sit down, and
I'll pour you a cup of coffee. Did you find Timmy?"

"Yes. He's got a new job at the truck stop."

The note in her voice made Aunt Jan pause, coffeepot
in hand. "He's had that a month now."

"Timmy never mentioned it to me." The new chasm
between Timmy and herself scared Margaret.

"Matt is a good role model for Timmy," Aunt Jan said.

"How are things in the restaurant?" Margaret asked quickly, in an effort to change the subject. She didn't want to talk about Matthew Magnum just yet.

"We're busy, but I wish we had more help. I told you about Gina, who works the cash register. Her baby is due in two weeks. I haven't found anyone to replace her yet, and I have one more vacancy to fill. The employment agency in Garrison has promised to keep a lookout for suitable help, but apparently working in a restaurant in Inchwater isn't everyone's ideal job."

The door between the restaurant and kitchen opened, and a girl in an advanced state of pregnancy entered. Seeing Margaret, she paused.

"Gina, come in and join us for a cup of coffee." Janet smiled at the girl. "This is Margaret, my niece. Margaret, this is Gina Wade."

"I don't want to interrupt," Gina said shyly. "I just wanted to thank you for that shepherd's pie you gave me yesterday, Janet. Jack loved it."

Some things never changed. Margaret and Timmy had a private theory that Aunt Jan gave away half the food she cooked.

"I've made some spaghetti sauce for you to take home tonight," Janet said. "Freeze it. It'll come in handy after the baby's here. Now, sit down before your break's over."

"Your aunt never stops talking about you," Gina told Margaret, sliding her bulk into a chair. "She's told me all about the work you do with physically handicapped children in Washington."

Margaret nodded. "I love my job. I only wish it was closer to home."

"The Edwards Institute is making a name for itself, slowly but surely," Aunt Jan said with pride.

"Who runs it?" Gina asked.

"Dr. Aaron Edwards," Margaret replied. "An article he read about children with birth defects who had been abandoned by their parents affected him deeply, and he gave up a successful practice to start the Institute. His aim was to take in as many children as he could and care for them. After a while he discovered some of the children benefited from being read to and taught. He hired teachers who would give them individual attention. I was teaching in San Francisco when I heard about his work, and wrote to him. Luckily for me, he hired me.''

"Teaching handicapped children must need a great deal of patience,'' Gina said, as she looked at Margaret over the rim of her coffee mug.

"I love my work,'' Margaret agreed.

"The secret of happiness is enjoying the work you do,'' Aunt Jan added. "It's a shame people pick careers for the money they'll make at it, instead of doing what they really want to.''

"Are you feeling all right?'' Margaret asked, noticing the sudden grimace on Gina's face.

"I'm fine. My back is just kind of sore.'' Gina finished her coffee and stood up, rubbing her back as she carried her mug to the sink. "Time to start working again. It was nice meeting you, Margaret.''

As Gina left, Margaret looked at her aunt. "She's very young, isn't she?''

Aunt Jan nodded. "Dropped out of school to get married when she found out she was pregnant. She's very reliable, though, and her husband is one of Matt's drivers.''

It appeared Matthew Magnum had woven himself into everyones's life in Inchwater. Abruptly Margaret stood up. "Do you need any help here?''

Aunt Jan shook her head. "I most certainly do not. Get some rest after that long flight. You look like death warmed over.''

Margaret gave her aunt a quick smile, and turned away. The stairs hugged the left exterior wall of the building and led to the living quarters upstairs: four bedrooms, three baths, a living room, a dining room and a tiny alcove kitchen, rarely used except for fixing hot beverages in the microwave.

Going straight to the bathroom adjoining her room, Margaret examined her reflection. Now she knew what death warmed over looked like. Dark circles ringed her caramel eyes, tension and exhaustion blanched the color from her face making every single freckle on her nose, and across her cheeks, stand out. Her curly, red, waist-length hair tied back in a single, thick braid looked lank and life-less. The suit she'd been in since yesterday looked rum-pled. Leaving D.C. right after the end-of-term staff meeting to catch her plane hadn't given Margaret time to change.

Margaret slipped out of her clothes and into the shower. Under the soothing hot water, her mind perked up enough to toss the experiences of the last few hours like a jug-gler's colored balls.

The man in the truck stop. So strong. So angry. Timmy looking at her as if he didn't like her. Aunt Jan's patient, strained face shining with love.

The picture stayed with Margaret while she toweled herself dry, slipped into a pair of cotton pajamas and got into bed. Seeing a truck stop in Inchwater had brought all her fears to the surface. Beneath her fear of Timmy work-ing around trucks was the other one, the one that shad-owed her days and haunted her nights. She was afraid death would snatch Timmy away from her, just as it had robbed her of her parents.

Stop it, you're too tired to think straight now.

Deliberately Margaret filled her mind with more pleas-ant pictures: Aunt Jan's smile, how nice it was to be back in her old room again. There would be time enough to sort out her thoughts later.

Chapter Two

"How's it going, Tim?" Matt asked as he watched the boy clean some tools.

The red head shot up and brown eyes exactly like Margaret Browning's looked at him. Only the expression in the eyes differed. She hadn't bothered to hide her hostility and tension yesterday, whereas Timmy looked friendly and happy, "Fine, Mr. Magnum."

"Is your sister home for the summer?"

He didn't miss the frown on the boy's face. "I don't know yet."

Matt recalled his remark about their mouths being different. Margaret Browning had a full lower lip and the upper was beautifully arched. Tim's had a determined tilt to it and none of the fullness.

"Been a while since she came home, hasn't it?" In the eighteen months he'd been in Inchwater, Matt hadn't seen hide nor hair of the gorgeous redhead. He'd heard her mentioned quite often, though.

"She usually comes home at Christmas." Tim bowed his head. "But last year we all took a cruise together. During the summer Margaret works in Washington, and Aunt Jan and I go there to spend time with her. She's got a neat apartment."

Matt's brows drew together. The sophisticated woman he had just met fitted perfectly into Washington society. Yet the look of pain in her eyes had hinted at soul-deep vulnerability.

"Well," Matt said, turning away, "if any of you need a ride into Los Angeles or Vegas for a shopping trip, you know my offer still holds good. Any of the drivers will be happy to take you."

"Thanks, Mr. Magnum, but Margaret doesn't like riding in trucks."

If Margaret Browning did not like riding in trucks, why had she stared at them as if transfixed? Matt wondered. He was quite sure he hadn't imagined the stunned expression on her face, or the dazed look in her eyes. He recalled Janet mentioning once that Timmy and Margaret's parents had been killed when their father had had a heart attack behind the wheel of his truck. Had being here raised the ghost of the past for Margaret Browning?

"Mr. Magnum," called a voice from the door of his office. "Tom Camden of T.C. Trucking wants to talk to you. He's holding on line one."

"Be right there." Matt shrugged. He had plenty to do other than psycho-analyze Tim Browning's sister.

"Let me know if you need extra time off while she's here."

"Yes, sir."

"Hi, sis! You didn't have to wait up for me," Timmy said as he entered the garden and found her sitting on the old swing.

Margaret smiled affectionately. "I thought we might talk."

"I'll grab a soda and be right back."

Waiting for him to come back from a date or a jaunt with his friends was a habit. Yesterday, her first night back, Margaret had fallen asleep early but today she had decided to wait for Timmy.

She and Timmy had often sat on the swing, talking late into the night. Here they didn't have to worry about disturbing Aunt Jan, who rose at five every morning. The garden, with its familiar scents and shadows, was a good place for exchanging secrets. The old swing creaked as it moved in the silent night, its rhythm comforting.

Margaret had no intention of settling down yet, not that there were a heap of men fighting to change her mind. She wanted to see Timmy through college first and ensure The Inner Man was at a stage where Aunt Jan had little else to do but supervise, before she could think of herself.

Timmy came out through the kitchen door, sat down opposite her and took a big gulp from the can in his hand. "So, what did you do today, sis?"

"I slept for most of the day, then unpacked and generally lazed around."

The rectangle of yellow light shining from the kitchen made it easy to notice Timmy's expression was carefully noncommittal. He ran his fingers through his hair, and she tensed. He only did that when he felt awkward.

"I thought we'd catch up on all the news," Margaret said with a smile.

"There isn't much to talk about."

Panic clutched at her. When had this close-mouthed stranger taken the place of her talkative brother? Aunt Jan always said she, Margaret, was the introvert in the family, Timmy the extrovert. To listen to him now, no one would suspect it.

"Are you planning to stay all summer?" Was it her imagination, or was there a sudden wariness to Timmy's tone?

"Yes."

Margaret had made the decision on the spur of the moment after the last time she had talked to Aunt Jan. Timmy, Aunt Jan had told her, planned to work through the summer. She herself wouldn't be able to come out to Washington this year because of lack of experienced help at the restaurant. Aunt Jan had sounded unlike herself, tired and dispirited, and Margaret had made up her mind to return to Inchwater and help her.

Aunt Jan had been thrilled by her decision. If Margaret's decision had the same effect on Timmy, he did an excellent job of not showing it. Keeping the smile on her face with difficulty, Margaret asked, "How do you like your new job?"

Timmy's face lit up. "Mr. Magnum's cool. He doesn't swear like Dan did. Plus, he's giving me twenty-five cents an hour more."

"That's great." Margaret's voice sounded hollow in her ears.

"How are things in Washington?" Timmy asked.

"Great." Why had she never realized before what an inane word it was?

"Do you have a part-time job lined up in Garrison for the summer?" Timmy asked.

"No." The Edwards Institute could not afford to pay teachers during the summer, and Margaret's part-time summer jobs had helped stretch her tight budget. "I'm going to help Aunt Jan in the restaurant. I just thought we would spend some time as a family this year…maybe take a trip to Yosemite."

The three of them had enjoyed previous visits to the National Park.

"That's great," Timmy said.

That word again. Since when had Timmy and she started using it so often with each other? Margaret wondered.

"I can't get the time off yet, though, but I think Aunt Jan will enjoy a trip to Yosemite. Mr. Magnum says I have the makings of a good mechanic, and if I want to, he's going to let me start going on short trips with the drivers."

No, screamed Margaret's mind, bucking to throw off the dark picture Timmy's words presented. *No.*

She didn't want Timmy involved in the trucking business as their father had been. She wanted Timmy to have a nice eight-to-five job and a settled family life.

Sounding calm took real effort. "How did you do on your preliminary SAT test last summer?"

The Scholastic Aptitude Test grades helped colleges determine who they would accept, and at Christmas Timmy had mentioned taking the SAT exam as many times as he could this year.

Timmy shrugged, "Okay. The Math is easy, but the English is really tough."

"I thought we might use part of the summer going over the comprehension part of the SAT manual. You know the higher the score you can get, the better your chances of getting into a good school are."

Timmy wanted to be an engineer, and Margaret wanted him to get into the finest engineering school in the country.

"I may not take the SAT exam, sis."

"What do you mean?" Lightning, scoring a direct hit, couldn't have frightened her more.

"I'm not sure if I want to go to college."

"N-not sure?"

"I think I just want to work full-time after I graduate, maybe go to truck driving school."

Maybe this was a nightmare brought on by too much worrying.

"T-truck driving school?" The fears she had dismantled as imaginary had a good solid foundation under them.

"Yes." Timmy stood up. "I have to be up early in the morning to go fishing with Matt. I said I'd show him the best place for trout. Good night, sis."

"'Night, Timmy."

He was going to show that stranger *their* stream, let him catch *their* trout, in nearby Garrison State Park. She didn't know what hurt more, the fact he hadn't asked her along, or the fact he was taking Matthew Magnum to their favorite spot. The man had to have made a really deep impression on Timmy. Deeper apparently, then she had, in all these years.

Margaret sat there, feeling very alone, dimly aware of the creak of the garden swing, of the smell of the herbs Aunt Jan planted each year, of her thoughts bouncing about in her head again. The chains that suspended the broad swing felt cold and hard under her fingers. The kitchen door opened, and she watched one of the late-shift employees carry a bag of trash to the bin at the side of the building. Everything seemed unreal. Resentment flooded Margaret as she thought of what Matthew Magnum's truck stop had done to her brother.

Timmy wanted to go to truck driving school. He wanted to drive a big rig . . . just like Daddy had. Pain was a vise clamping down on Margaret's heart. She felt the way she had when they'd told her her parents were never coming back. Life was once again spinning out of control. Margaret knew she had to do something about it as soon as possible.

The asphalt was wet when she stepped on it a week later. Though she had made up her mind to talk to Matthew Magnum the second day she had been in Inchwater, she hadn't picked up the courage to do it until now. Margaret told herself it was because she had been busy helping in the restaurant this past week.

A couple of truckers, on the way to their rigs, glanced at her curiously. Margaret knew she looked out of place dressed in a skirt and a cotton sweater, a silk scarf draped around her neck. She needed the confidence her semi-formal outfit would give her for this meeting. Even her unruly hair had been put up to emphasize the businesslike nature of her visit.

Unable to reach Matthew Magnum on the telephone the day before yesterday, the message she'd left on his machine had been answered by a girl who said she was his part-time office assistant. Mr. Magnum would be happy to see her at seven, Wednesday morning. Timmy reported for work at eight, so that, Margaret thought, should give her plenty of time for what she wanted to say.

"May I help you?" A woman looked up from the computer on her desk as Margaret walked into the office.

Tugging at the hem of her pink sweater, Margaret said, "I'm looking for Mr. Magnum. Matthew Magnum. Is he here?"

"He's in the building at the back. Last room on your left as you face it."

"Thank you."

Margaret walked toward the building on legs that were suddenly shaky. Her gaze swerved to the left, went past the last door and then stopped. Incredibly enough, among all the concrete and vehicles, someone had cleared an area twelve feet square and built a two-foot brick wall around it. The space inside was covered with emerald green grass, and a jacaranda tree in the middle had shed a design of flowers. Lining the bricks were a variety of rose bushes blooming profusely. The fragrance of the roses permeated the air. It was a strange place for a garden, and yet the sheer beauty of it touched Margaret. She wondered who had thought of setting it here.

The roar of an engine was an abrupt reminder she wasn't here to admire the place, but simply to meet the owner, and she'd better get on with it.

Turning to the door on her left, she looked at the name plate. Magnum, it stated simply, with no embellishments.

"Come in." The answer to her knock made Margaret push the door open cautiously.

He was staring out the window. Margaret took in the stool he sat on, and the old desk covered with piles of paper. From where she stood, she could see the office overlooked the little garden.

She'd expected this room to match the front office, something like the corporate offices one saw on television with a huge, impressive desk, a plush, leather armchair, a gorgeous, blond secretary. Besides the table with coffee supplies and a few folding chairs, this one held ordinary bookshelves and filing cabinets. Another table, against a far wall, held a computer and a printer. There was little else in the room. The words that jumped into Margaret's mind as she looked around were warm, simple, *homey*.

The crackle of voices in the background told her Matthew Magnum was listening to a CB radio. Perking coffee filled the room with a delicious morning smell. Margaret couldn't help noticing his dark hair was shower damp.

The fact he was looking at the garden made her pause. Had the rose garden been Matthew Magnum's idea? The thought was unsettling. The impression she had of a tough, impatient man was at odds with the one she received now. This ordinary room and the garden were like little peepholes into his mind. What she saw confused her. Margaret could deal with tough and impatient, she had met many men like that, but the latter... the latter made her uneasy, hinting here was something very likable, very human about Matthew Magnum. She tried to push away the feeling.

Margaret swallowed, trying to get her thoughts under control. "Mr. Magnum...."

He swung around, his gaze swept her from head to toe, and then he got to his feet. Faded jeans molded his long legs, a blue-and-white checked shirt had sleeves rolled up to just above the elbows, exposing arms covered with a smattering of dark hair. The cleft in his chin looked deeper and more dangerous than ever.

"Ah! Tim Browning's sister. Lexi said you wanted to see me. What can I do for you?"

Margaret's breath caught in her throat. Matthew Magnum's question increased her uneasiness. The scent of pine wrapped her, flushing confusion where momentary calm had been. He towered over her like a California redwood, and she stepped back and tilted her head so she could look at him better.

"First of all, I want to apologize for jaywalking the last time I was here." That was better. Her voice was steady, her words according to plan. Disarm first, and then attack. "The second reason I'm here is to talk to you about Timmy."

Picking up a pile of papers from a folding chair, Matthew Magnum dumped them on the ground. "Have a seat." Switching the radio off, he turned another chair around and sat astride it.

Margaret sat gingerly on the edge of her chair and took another deep breath. This wasn't the rational discussion she'd visualized. There was something disconcerting in the way Matthew Magnum sat astride the chair, the fact he was only three feet away. The morning light made his eyes seem different today... green mixed with yellow, like newly budding leaves in spring. The look in them was far from formal as he scrutinized her appearance. The half smile on his face drew attention to his chin and made her forget what she wanted to say. Margaret wet her lips. She had to remain calm or nothing would go the way she'd planned it. One hand came up and started wrapping the end of her silk scarf around her fingers.

"Would you like some coffee?"

"No, thank you." She hoped the shake of her head was determined enough to prevent any further interruptions. "I just want a few minutes of your time."

"Sure."

She licked her lips. "Timmy is very young. Teenagers often go through phases that don't really mean anything. If you wouldn't encourage him in this..."

Her voice trailed off. She was making a mess of things. Her words weren't making sense even to her.

"What exactly am I encouraging him in?"

Margaret twisted the soft silk of her scarf with nervous hands. "This fascination with trucks. Timmy's going to be an engineer."

"Why?" The word dropped like a stone into the whirlpool of her confusion.

"He looks up to you. All he talks of is Mr. Magnum this, or Mr. Magnum that...." Last night during supper Timmy had kept on and on about his new job, not noticing that her enthusiasm hadn't matched his.

"That isn't what I meant." There was nothing in his voice to show he was flattered by Tim's adulation. "I mean why does he *have* to be an engineer?"

She tried to rephrase that. "My father was a trucker. Both my parents were killed when he had a heart attack behind the wheel, and his truck crashed."

"So as long as your brother doesn't become a trucker, he'll be safe?" She hadn't noticed what a stern nose he had before. The flaring nostrils expressed disapproval clearly.

"You don't know what this will do to Aunt Jan." Margaret couldn't keep the quiver out of her voice. A quiver of anger, not helplessness. The scarf was crushed in one fist now.

Matt leaned against the old desk. "Why don't you tell me what it will do to Janet? She knows Tim works with me, and she has no objections."

Margaret couldn't hold her next words back. "She probably hopes, like I do, that this is some passing whim of Timmy's. I don't want her to relive the trauma associated with trucking in her life."

"If there was any trauma associated with trucking in her mind, I doubt if Janet would have opened a restaurant for truckers."

As she stared at him, Margaret realized she had made a mistake coming here. He was enjoying arguing with her. Nothing she said was going to make a difference. She stood, pushing the folding chair away from under her. "I won't take up any more of your time, Mr. Magnum."

Matt put his hand out and gently held her, just above her elbow.

"Don't."

"Excuse me?" Her voice sounded sad and vulnerable. Matt felt a tightening in his gut, a response to the child he glimpsed in the woman.

"Don't run out there with tears blurring your vision. I don't want you stepping in front of one of my trucks in this condition." His thumb roved the surface of the skin inside her elbow and he felt her go very still.

Matt could tell she was both angry and nervous. He watched her crumple the scarf in her fist and heard a small sniff before she said sharply, "I cry when I'm angry."

Moving away from her, Matt threw her a glance over his shoulder. "Why are you angry? Because you're not getting your way for once?"

"It's not that," she said angrily. "It's because I can't bear the thought of Timmy being a trucker."

"Cream? Sugar?"

She stared at him for a minute, and Matt thought she was going to slam her way out of the office or throw something at him. As he watched, she lifted her chin and said stubbornly, "I don't want any coffee."

"It will help you calm down. Besides, we haven't finished our discussion yet." If Tim Browning was an open book, his sister was so tightly closed and bound it would need more than words to get through to her. It would need time.

"A little cream and one sugar please." The lack of cordiality in her voice didn't bother him.

Granted losing her parents had been hard on Margaret Browning, but that was no excuse for taking over her brother's life as if the boy had no mind of his own. Matt's brows drew together as he remembered his own father's determination to tailor his life, the fight he'd had to put up for his freedom.

He handed her one of the cups and said, "Tim is old enough to make his own decisions."

"He's only sixteen," she said defensively.

"Isn't that the same age you were when you graduated from high school, and left home to attend college?"

How on earth did he know their entire family history? Margaret blinked. It was true. She had skipped two grades in elementary school and graduated two years ahead of others her age, so she had been sixteen when she'd left home for Berkeley.

"Girls are more mature than boys the same age."

"Individual cases vary," he returned calmly. "What is it that Tim says he wants to do?"

"He mentioned t-truck driving school, instead of college." It was hard even to get the words out.

Matthew Magnum frowned. "I may be partly responsible for that decision. We talked the other day about life on the road, and I might have led him to think he could earn fifty thousand dollars. I didn't realize Tim would opt for a career in trucking before college, though."

"F-fifty thousand dollars?" It was more than she earned as a teacher, with five years of college and a degree in education. Their father had certainly never earned that amount.

"Who do you think you are, filling his head with lies?" Margaret asked angrily.

Lightning flashed in Matthew Magnum's eyes. "I don't deal in lies, Ms. Browning. I have five truckers on my payroll earning that amount, and two who earn seventy-five thousand a year."

"It isn't the norm."

"Exactly what I was about to say. These men have been with Bedouin Trucking for years, and they're excellent, reliable, long-distance drivers. It takes an average of thirty years in the business to get where they are now."

"There's no guarantee that Tim will ever get to that stage."

"Just as there's no guarantee he'll ever make a good engineer."

"He'll be *safe* as an engineer."

"What do you base that assumption on? Is there some medical survey that shows engineers don't have heart attacks and die at forty-three?"

It was no use talking to a man who couldn't see farther than the end of his nose. Margaret took a big gulp of coffee, in a hurry to finish it. In a hurry to leave.

"The problem as I see it here is not him, but you."

She was the problem. This was really great. "What do you mean?" Her voice held open hostility.

"You've got this cage for your brother. It's labeled *engineer* and *safe,* and you want to coax him into it with no thought of his feelings. Granted you're motivated by love, and it's a gilded cage, but that's no excuse for what you're doing."

Margaret felt her jaw go slack. Who did Matthew Magnum think he was, analyzing her as if she were on a psychiatrist's couch in his office?

"You barely spend two weeks a year here at Christmas," Matt continued. "Tim visits you during the summer for another couple of weeks. On an association of four weeks a year, how can you think you know what's best for him? You don't even know what's best for yourself."

Margaret swallowed hard and opened her mouth, but no words emerged.

"Have you thought about it from Timmy's point of view?"

Margaret shook her head.

"This isn't easy for him," Matt said. "From what he's said indirectly when we've talked, he's worried about how you'll react to his working here. He's very close to you...don't do anything to ruin your relationship with him."

"I care too much about my brother to stand by and let him make a mess of his life."

The granite chin seemed to become even harder. "This isn't even about Timmy's job, is it? It's about control. You're losing control over your brother and that's what frightens you the most."

Margaret's hand clenched into a fist. "I don't know what you mean."

"Oh, yes, you do," Matt said sternly, "so don't pretend otherwise. You've always controlled Timmy and you want to continue to control him."

"I want what's best for Timmy."

"That's a poor reason." Matt swung away from her to stare out of his window. "I know how harmful your kind of dominance is. My father never listened to what I wanted out of life. He was autocratic in his decisions where his children were concerned and each of us left home as soon as we could. Unless you change, you'll lose your brother."

A frisson of fear swept through Margaret. "Timmy's too young to know what he wants."

Matthew Magnum didn't seem to hear her. "He's not too young to know what he wants. I was fifteen when I ran away from home to get away from my father. Luckily for me, I met someone who talked some sense into me and made me return. My life could have turned out very different otherwise. In Timmy I see the boy I was, confused, frustrated, stubborn. You both seem to share the last trait. If you don't change your outlook you're going to lose him."

"I am not trying to control Timmy's life, only..."

"*Only* his decision to work here, then it will be *only* the college he goes to, then *only* the woman he marries. Timmy's not a pawn on your chessboard."

The man was beyond reasoning with. Why had she ever thought coming here would help matters?

Even as she stared at him, he said, "For the record, I have nothing to do with Timmy's decision not to go to college. I encourage every employee of mine to get all the education they can."

Margaret looked around, found a trash can, and carefully dropped her cup into it. Positioning the strap of her bag on her shoulder with the utmost care, she said formally, "Goodbye, Mr. Magnum."

She stalked out of the office, her head buzzing with fury. One jarring word more, and she was going to explode. Halfway home, Margaret ran out of names to call him. Anger still at a rapid boil, she walked into the kitchen of The Inner Man.

"Good morning, Margaret. You're up early."

Margaret picked up a plate, put a warm bran muffin on it, poured herself a mug of milk and was partway up the stairs before she realized she hadn't returned Aunt Jan's greeting.

Banging the door to her room shut, she placed her hastily collected breakfast on the dresser and flung herself on her bed.

Drat Matthew Magnum. Drat Timmy. Drat everybody.

Margaret lay there for a long while, lost in the memories jostling each other in her mind.

Daddy brushing her hair with those great big hands of his, awkwardly wielding her tiny brush as he said, "All princesses have long hair." Mommy pushing her on the swing, smiling down at her. Daddy lifting her in the hospital, so she could look at her baby brother. Mommy telling her she was the big sister; it was her job to take care of Timmy when they were away.

The memories hurt. Hurt all the more because Timmy didn't have any. Timmy hadn't had time to get a collection of them together, like she had, before their parents died. She had tried to make it up to him…they all had, but it wasn't the same. Margaret swallowed the lump in her throat. All she wanted was Timmy's happiness.

She remembered the funeral clearly, remembered Aunt Jan holding her as she cried, whispering into her ear, "It's all right. We'll manage."

But it hadn't been all right. For months, she had cried herself to sleep. Aunt Jan had worked very hard to drown out her own grief, while filling the hole that the loss of their parents had left in Margaret and Timmy's lives.

No, she didn't want Timmy following in her father's footsteps. And he wouldn't have thought of it, if Mr. Know-it-all Magnum hadn't come to Inchwater.

Margaret sat up abruptly. Why was she allowing Matthew Magnum to get to her like this, anyway? He wasn't important. Timmy was. She would let the matter lie for a few days, then bring it up again, make him see where his prospects were brightest. Timmy would come around. He always had before.

Chapter Three

Margaret changed into shorts and a camisole top, and went downstairs. Working would keep her from worrying about Timmy.

"Aunt Jan, do you know what brings Matthew Magnum to Inchwater? Joe said something, but I can't quite remember what," Margaret asked, entering the kitchen.

Her aunt paused to adjust the temperature of the electric oven and glance at Annie, the girl helping her in the kitchen. Assuring herself the chicken legs were being rolled in the breadcrumbs in just the right manner, she said, "Well, that's why you were so preoccupied. Matt came here eighteen months ago, when he bought the land from old Harvey Simms. When he started construction he came here off and on to keep an eye on things. Once the truck stop went into operation, he started spending most of his time here though his headquarters are in Los Angeles."

"But what's he *still* doing here?" Surely, it didn't take more than a few days to check things out. Inchwater was no Shangri-la for visitors.

Janet shrugged as she slid a batch of chicken legs into the oven. "He says he likes it here. It's quiet, the pace is slow and people have time for each other."

Margaret wondered why no one had mentioned the truck stop to her. Between her weekly telephone conversations with Aunt Jan and Timmy, and the regular letters Aunt Jan wrote, very little went on in Inchwater that Margaret didn't know about. Yet both of them had avoided mentioning Bedouin Trucking or Matthew Magnum. Had the silent conspiracy been based on the surmise that what she didn't know wouldn't hurt her?

"He isn't *staying* in Inchwater is he?"

People who praised Inchwater were generally the kind passing through who stopped to take pictures of the sunsets, secure in the knowledge they'd never have to live here for good. If they had to stay somewhere, they usually chose Garrison which had more to offer in the way of accommodation and things to do. It was where she expected Matthew Magnum to be staying.

Aunt Jan nodded absently as she looked around for something. "He has a room at Mac's motel. Says he wants to be close to the truck stop as he works odd hours. Matt did mention he might consider having a house built here later if he decides to stay in Inchwater permanently."

Inchwater had no other motels or houses for rent. Mac's motel was the only choice for anyone wanting to stay here. Lumpy mattresses, televisions that didn't work and occasional running hot water. Matthew Magnum deserved it all. "How did Timmy meet him?"

"Matt's been a frequent customer in the restaurant, but Timmy didn't really meet him till Matt was invited to Garrison High, to talk to the juniors and seniors during career week. After that, Timmy asked Matt so many questions, Matt invited him to visit the truck stop. The next thing I knew, Matt had hired Timmy."

Aunt Jan glanced at her niece's still face and then said, "The truck stop is a much better place for Timmy to work in than Dan's Donuts. Dan has a mouth that would need a ton of laundry detergent to get clean, and the other boy he's hired has a police record."

Matthew Magnum wouldn't last through July and August, Margaret told herself, when the hot winds blew from the desert, coating Inchwater in dust. Boredom would soon drive him away, and then she would have her brother back. Working at the truck stop was just a phase Timmy was passing through.

"Matt has been very nice," Aunt Jan said. "Nowadays, truck stops have cafés besides stores, fuel pumps, repair services and a place for the truckers to sleep and shower. If he had added a café to his truck stop, I would have had to close down for lack of business. One of the first things he did was reassure me he would do no such thing."

Aunt Jan was right about that, Margaret conceded. The Inner Man's customers were eighty percent truckers and there wasn't enough business to support yet another restaurant.

"Do you need help in here?" Margaret asked Aunt Jan as Jan turned to the oven.

"No. If you don't have anything else to do, why don't you relieve Gina at the cash register?"

Margaret smiled. "You mean get out of your way don't you, Aunt Jan? See you later."

She slipped into the restaurant and waited until Gina had rung up a customer's bill to ask, "How are you feeling, Gina?"

Gina gave her a huge smile. "Hi, Margaret! I'm fine. All I ask is that Junior stop football practice till he gets out. Jack says we don't have to worry about paying the kid's college tuition...at the rate Junior's kicking, he'll definitely get a sports scholarship."

The cash register was one of the newfangled ones that did everything except hand back the change. Margaret had quickly gotten used to it. What she found hard was being around the truckers who made up the majority of The Inner Man's customers. Their special slang, their mannerisms and their clothes brought back poignant memories of her parents.

Even as a child Margaret had avoided the restaurant for that reason. Later, as a teenager, she'd preferred catching a bus to Garrison to work in a fabric store, rather than the diner. Now, what with the truck stop and the hours she would put in behind the register, Margaret felt her memories were in danger of overexposure.

Gina picked up her bag and yawned. "Excuse me. I seem to be very sleepy lately. I'm glad you're helping out in the restaurant. I've stopped feeling guilty about leaving when the baby's born. Janet was worried that not a single person answered her ad for a cashier."

"People like working in Garrison or Barstow better."

Gina nodded as she slid off the chair behind the register. "Janet said that's one of the reasons she converted the place to a self-service restaurant. This way she can manage with fewer employees."

Margaret took Gina's place behind the register, her attention already fixed on the customer waiting to pay his bill. The job wasn't hard. So far, no one had started a conversation with her, which suited her, although Gina always found something to talk about with each customer.

Margaret wondered if her princess look did the trick for her. Her colleagues at the Edwards Institute said that when she had it in place, they knew better than to bother her. Very few people knew the aloof look was made up of both shyness and nervousness.

Janet Hooper looked up as she heard a sound at the back door.

"Matt!" she greeted the visitor. "Did you smell my apple pie all the way to your truck stop?"

Cutting a huge piece of hot pie she slid it onto a plate. "Sit, and have that while I get your check. You haven't been around in a while."

"There's no hurry for the money, Janet," Matt said quickly.

Janet shook her head. "You were kind enough to give me an interest-free loan when I needed it, besides allowing me to repay you in easy installments. I'm not going to be lax about paying you back."

"Your niece left her scarf at the truck stop last week, and I just came by to return it," Matt said, sitting down and reaching for the pie.

Janet looked up from the check she was writing. "Margaret came by to see you? This wouldn't be last Wednesday, would it?"

Matt nodded, but didn't elaborate.

Janet paused to take her glasses off and pinch the bridge of her nose. "She seemed upset that day. She's very close to Timmy. I knew it would upset Margaret to find out he was working at the truck stop. Did you tell her the boy Timmy had started hanging out with had a police record?"

Matt shook his head. "No."

Jan held the check out to him. "Matt, I know I've never mentioned this before, but could you please not tell Margaret about the loan?"

"She won't hear about it from me, but why do you feel you have to shield her from the truth? You've had a very hard time this last year, and she's old enough to know about it." It was that look, Matt supposed. That little-girl-lost look had gotten to him, as well.

Janet sat down and looked at him. "I'm not trying to shield her. If Margaret knows about the loan, she'll insist on withdrawing her savings and repaying you, and I don't want that."

"Your niece means a great deal to you, doesn't she Janet?" Matt said, recalling Janet Hooper's expression when she had told him Margaret was coming home for a visit.

Janet nodded. "Margaret's had a great deal of problems to confront all her life, Matt. With the exception of her brother and myself, she has never let anyone matter to her. It's as if she doesn't want anything to distract her from taking care of Timmy."

Matt cleared his throat, wondering if Janet's opinion of her niece wasn't colored by her love for Margaret. "Doesn't she earn a good salary in Washington? She should be helping you out financially."

Janet stared at him in surprise. "Margaret is the most generous person in this family. She can't help me out because she took a loan to put herself through college, and she had to repay it as soon as she started working. The Edwards Institute cannot afford to pay teachers much, which is why Margaret usually finds another job during the summer to stretch her finances. Last year, she gave us a wonderful cruise as a Christmas gift because she knew I've always wanted to go on one. She's saving for Timmy's college now, so that he won't have to apply for financial aid like she did. She's always sending us things and..."

"Enough!" Matt held both hands up in a gesture of surrender. He knew when he had lost. It was obvious that in Janet's eyes her niece could do no wrong. He picked up the scarf. "I think I'll return this to her myself."

A sound at the door brought Margaret's head up. She stiffened. The huge frame in the doorway obliterated the light for a few seconds, long enough to start her heart thudding, before Matthew Magnum stepped forward.

"Your property, I believe."

He dropped the scarf in a heap on the counter, and Margaret stared at it, mesmerized. The last time she'd seen it was when she'd worn it to her meeting with him.

"You left it behind in my office. It must have slid behind the desk. I found it this morning when a paper went over the edge."

Margaret felt her face grow hot. "Thank you for bringing it back." It hurt to be grateful to him, and the words stuck in her throat, but the Italian silk scarf had been a graduation present from Aunt Jan, and manners were important.

"I thought of something after you left the other day, and if you aren't too busy, maybe we could talk." His gaze shifted to a spot behind her, "Gina, could you take over and let Margaret have a break?"

Margaret turned her head to see Gina standing at her elbow, looking apologetic. "I'm sorry I took so long again, Margaret. I fell asleep."

"Don't worry about it. You need the rest."

"I certainly got it, thanks to you."

"Margaret?" Matthew had collected two mugs from the counter and filled them with coffee.

Reluctantly, Margaret got to her feet.

Matt looked at her as she came out from behind the counter. One eyebrow lifted as he took in her denim shorts. He gave a silent whistle at the long, shapely legs below them and the way her clothes clung to her curves. Her red hair was tied back, but curls escaped to frame her face and kiss her nape. Her gaze met his. Margaret looked away quickly, but not before he'd seen her reluctance to have anything to do with him.

He couldn't explain why he wanted to see her again. He could have given the scarf to Timmy or even left it with Janet, but since his meeting with her last week he hadn't been able to get his mind off Margaret Browning. He told himself he was concerned about Timmy, but it had been Margaret's face that had occupied his thoughts all week. He wanted to find out more about her, get past the tight self-control.

They slipped into one of the window booths, and Margaret watched Matthew Magnum put a spoonful of sugar and a little cream into one of the mugs, before placing it in front of her.

"Just how you like it."

Was that a teasing note she heard in his voice? "Thanks." The word came out stiff and awkward, the way she felt around him.

Picking up a teaspoon, Margaret stirred her coffee vigorously, wondering what he wanted to discuss. They had nothing in common, except Timmy. Strangely enough, a picture of Matthew Magnum's garden popped into her mind.

The prolonged silence forced her into an opening remark. "It's a nice day, isn't it?"

There was something so serious about her, so *earnest*. Had no one told Margaret Browning caring for oneself was as important as caring for others? Maybe, thought Matt, she needed help shedding the cocoon she had wrapped herself in all these years.

"It is a nice day," he said. "It was last week, also, but we forgot to mention it then. It was nice yesterday, too. Forecast says it's going to be nice tomorrow as well."

Provoking someone was foreign to his nature, but when he saw the expression in her eyes change, Matt was glad. Margaret needed to be provoked right out of her tight, little shell.

He definitely *was* laughing at her. Margaret felt her face tighten as he leaned toward her and said, "I came to apologize, Margaret."

"Apologize?" she asked coolly.

"For my remark about you being a prodigal. I was under the mistaken impression that you could help Jan financially, but chose not to. I had no call to make such assumptions, but I did, and I'm sorry."

Margaret stared at him, more impressed by the apology than she had been by anything else about Matthew Magnum. Admitting one's mistakes took courage. Most people she knew would rather ignore them.

"It doesn't matter," she said stiffly. What mattered was that he had been absolutely right in the other things he had said. She did want to nudge Timmy toward a safe job.

As if he read her thoughts Magnum asked, "Have you had time to think about the discussion we had last week?"

Margaret's temper blazed. "That was no discussion. You lectured and I listened, but that doesn't mean I agreed with everything you said. I'm not going to let you brainwash me. I love Timmy and want what's best for him."

"What *you* think is best for him," corrected Matt. "Janet mentioned you care so deeply about Timmy that you won't let anyone or anything distract you from your duty toward your brother. What do you plan, Margaret? To wait till Tim is safely married to someone you introduce him to, before thinking of your own future?"

Margaret took a deep breath. This man wasn't simply encroaching on her personal space. He was in the middle of it. Attack was sometimes the best form of defence. "Is it very boring for you here in Inchwater, Mr. Magnum?" she said. "Is that why you are taking such a personal interests in everybody's lives?"

"Call me Matt, Margaret. Inchwater is a lot of things, but I wouldn't call it boring."

"What would you call it?"

The hand that came up to cover hers made Margaret aware she was still stirring her coffee. She swallowed as the hand was casually removed and Matt said, "I like the solitude, the away-from-it-all atmosphere."

"There's nothing to do here."

"Is that why you stayed away for so long, Margaret, except for your brief visits at Christmas?"

He *did* know their entire family history. She dropped her gaze to her cup. "Work kept me away."

"Strange. Work is exactly what brought me here."

"How long will you be staying?"

She expected anger at her blunt question. Instead, he gave her a whimsical smile. "That would be a very flattering question, if you could only look a little wistful while you asked it."

Angry with the way her heart responded to the intensity in Matt's green eyes, Margaret snapped, "I'm not some gullible idiot to be lured by your smooth talk, Mr. Magnum."

"Pity." Matt stood, placed a tip beside his mug and glanced at her. "I would certainly like to lure you, Margaret Browning. Very much. I think we would both learn a great deal in the process. See you around."

He was gone before she'd cleared the shock from her system enough to find her voice.

I would certainly like to lure you, Margaret Browning.

She drew in a deep breath. Why that...that...wolf! He surely didn't think she was going to be taken in, as Timmy had been, did he?

Had he carried the teasing a little too far? Matt wondered. The flash of fear he had seen in her eyes at his last comment had shaken him. Helping Margaret Browning put herself first was one thing, but he'd better be careful he didn't get tangled up in the web of plans he was spinning. There was something about her melted chocolate eyes that got to him in a way nothing else ever had.

Two days later Margaret entered the restaurant at noon, took one look at Gina and said, "Gina, what's wrong?"

But she knew. There was a line of sweat on Gina's forehead, and the hand that clamped down on hers was icy cold.

"It's Junior. He wants out."

Stay calm, Margaret.

"Are you sure?"

Gina nodded. "I've had slight contractions all morning. I ignored them because I'm not due yet, but they're strong and unmistakable now."

"Don't worry, everything's going to be fine," Margaret said automatically. "I'll drive you to the hospital and stay with you till Jack gets there. Ben," she flung at the boy behind the counter, "get Aunt Jan."

Her aunt took over at once, asking Gina questions about contractions and water, while Margaret ran out to the car the family used for errands. She'd better start it before she got Gina into it. Sometimes the old engine refused to cooperate.

"Come on! Come on! Don't go temperamental on us now," Margaret urged, as the car remained stubbornly unresponsive.

"Need a ride?"

She looked at the shadow that fell across her. She might have known the omnipotent Matthew Magnum would be at hand. Still, this wasn't the time to let personal feelings get in the way. "It's Gina. She's in labor, and Beelzebub won't start."

"Beelzebub?"

She was already out, shutting the door. "The car," she said impatiently. "Where's yours? Can you take Gina to Garrison Community Hospital?"

"Over there."

His car was parked next to hers. Beside the silver-gray lines of the luxury automobile, Beelzebub looked like a giant bumblebee with its bright yellow body and black hood. "I'll get Gina."

"Whoa!" The hand on her shoulder burned her skin. "I'm not taking the lady in alone. Someone has to ride with us in case she decides to give birth en route."

About to argue that Gina would do no such thing, Margaret stopped. She didn't know anyone else who could get her from calm to storm in less than twenty seconds. Convincing this man of anything was a waste of time.

"I'll come," she snapped, hurrying in.

For a moment, she toyed with the idea of asking Aunt Jan to go in her place. Aunt Jan, who had been with their mother both at Margaret's and Timmy's births, knew all about having babies. Margaret opened her mouth and closed it again. It wasn't a feasible idea. The lunch rush was still on, and by four o'clock, early diners would be stopping in. Aunt Jan was the only person who could run The Inner Man.

"There's nothing to worry about," Aunt Jan told them all as she helped Gina out to the car. "The contractions are a good twenty minutes apart, and it takes only ten minutes to get to Garrison."

Margaret slipped into the back seat beside Gina, held her hand and tried to sound positive. "You're going to be fine."

Her face pale, Gina rested her head against the back of the seat and closed her eyes. "I only wish Jack wasn't out of town."

Margaret froze. Did Gina mean out of town, as in wouldn't-be-here-to-help? Aunt Jan hadn't mentioned anyone else in Gina's family. Which left her, Margaret, as the last resort.

She blinked rapidly. As last resort, she definitely wasn't in the running for any prizes.

Chapter Four

"Where is Jack?" Matt threw Gina a glance over his shoulder.

Gina's breath caught in her throat as pain washed through her like a wave.

"Short, shallow breaths," Margaret instructed, hoping it was the right thing to do at this stage of labor. It was what people said on television, anyway.

As Gina relaxed, Matt asked again, "Do you know which run Jack is on?"

"Barstow to Vegas."

"I see."

Margaret stared at the back of Matthew Magnum's dark head, resisting the urge to hit him. She doubted if he saw anything. Not Gina's need to have her husband with her. Not her own terror and ignorance.

This, she wanted to scream at him, *is what happens to men who become truckers. Their families suffer, their wives give birth alone and afraid. Now, do you see why I don't want this kind of life for Timmy?*

If looks could kill, Matthew Magnum would have fallen down dead right there, but they couldn't, so the car continued to purr smoothly as it covered the distance between Inchwater and Garrison.

Gina shifted and then said, her voice fraught with worry, "The baby's early. I hope he's going to be fine."

"How early?" Matt asked.

"Two weeks." There was a quaver of fear in Gina's voice.

"Probably just a slight miscalculation of when you actually became pregnant. Same thing happened to one of my sisters."

He sounded very confident, but then he wasn't the one having the baby, was he?

Margaret knew she was the most nervous of the three. This was the first time she had seen anyone in labor. She was trained to face emergencies calmly. She could handle a schoolyard fight, cut knees, even a broken hand. But this . . . this was something so different, she had no idea if she had what it took to help Gina. Scarlett O'Hara, she was definitely not.

Margaret looked up straight into Matt's eyes. Watchful, smiling, *reassuring*. He winked at her in the rearview mirror, and she felt her face grow hot.

"Gina, when was your last checkup?"

Matt's calm attitude had the right effect on Gina. She gave a small smile and said, "I saw Dr. Reddy last Thursday. He said everything looked fine."

"There, you see?" he said reassuringly. "There's nothing to worry about."

Gina sat up suddenly. "Oh, no! I forgot all about picking up my suitcase and the baby's bag from the apartment."

"I'll pick them up once we have you settled in the hospital." He pulled up at the Emergency entrance and said,

"Wait here while I get someone to bring out a wheelchair."

"My water hasn't broken," Gina fretted aloud as they waited.

What, Margaret wondered helplessly, happened if the water didn't break?

Matt took care of filling in the forms as Gina supplied the information, and then Gina was wheeled away with Margaret trotting anxiously beside her. Matt decided to pick up Gina's things and return quickly. He had a feeling both women would need him in the next few hours.

A nurse came forward, and Gina's grip on Margaret's hand tightened. "Don't leave me."

"Of course not." Margaret's heart sank, though her tone remained cheerful. She had an idea Gina wanted her to stay to the finish. Not outside in the waiting room, either. Right beside her. Margaret felt her palms dampen, her mouth go dry.

Waiting in the hallway while a doctor examined Gina, Margaret wondered where Matt had gone. She was sure it was the thrust of that determined chin, the glint of authority in the green eyes, that had gotten them through the tedious admitting details so quickly.

"You may go in now."

Margaret walked into the room. Gina, draped in a hospital gown, looked scared but managed a shaky smile. "Dr. Reddy said it's going to be about three hours before Junior makes his grand entrance."

"Well," Margaret said, borrowing some of the confidence she had heard in Matt's voice earlier. "That will give you a little time to give me a crash course in Lamaze. I don't think they'll let me stay if they know how green I am at all this."

Gina's smile wavered. "Jack attended the classes with me. We planned it so we would be together when Junior was born. He was going to take two weeks off at the end of this month."

"It's a good thing you're so well prepared for this baby." Margaret forced her voice to remain cheerful, though her heart ached for the young woman in the bed. Jack should have been there with Gina. As a substitute, she was the worst kind. Unprepared, inadequate, *ignorant*.

"We weren't prepared, really. Not at first. You know, Jack and I got married during our last year of school." Gina's voice came out slowly. "I was already pregnant, and we were scared because we had no money, no jobs, nothing. We hated living with my parents. Then someone mentioned looking for work in Inchwater, and I caught the bus there one day after Jack had left on another interview. Luckily, Janet took me on right away as kitchen assistant. I was too scared to tell her I was pregnant, and I thought she'd fire me when she found out, but instead Janet switched me to the cash register and gave me a note for Jack to take to Bedouin Trucking. Matt was in town for a brief visit, and he interviewed and hired him. He even paid for Jack to attend truck driving school in Barstow. It seemed like a miracle. Suddenly, we had everything. Money, a job, medical insurance. I could have regular prenatal checkups. The best part was finding a place of our own in Inchwater."

"I'm glad it all turned out so well," Margaret said.

"Not all teenagers in our situation are so lucky," said Gina soberly. "I went back to talk to the kids at Garrison High and shared our story with them. I wish someone had given us the facts, the way I gave it to them. Love doesn't stand a chance, unless you have an education and the means to support yourself."

Gina looked up at Margaret and said, "Am I boring you?"

Margaret shook her head. "It's fascinating." Talking was also better than waiting in silence for the next contraction.

"I'm going to get my high school diploma after the baby's here," Gina said, determination in her voice. "Then I've decided to take a secretarial course. My children aren't going to have a high school dropout for a mother."

Gina leaned forward as another contraction swept through her. "Ooh."

Margaret rubbed Gina's back, feeling helpless, wishing she could do more. Time them, the nurse had said, so she looked at her watch. Two fifteen.

The next one came fifteen minutes later, and it was barely over when the nurse bustled in.

"How are you doing?" she asked cheerfully.

"Fifteen minutes apart," Margaret said weakly.

"Fine," Gina replied in a bright, clear voice.

"Good." Reaching for Gina's wrist to check her pulse, the nurse looked at Margaret. "The hunk that brought you in is outside and wants to see you."

"Matt," Gina said.

Right away Matt noticed how pale Margaret was. Damp tendrils of hair clung to her neck, and her forehead glistened with the sheen of perspiration.

"I've brought Gina's things." He smiled as he handed her the bag and watched the color rise in her face. "How is she?"

"In a great deal of pain, and I have no idea what to do." Margaret's voice tugged at him. It held one part worry, two parts pathos.

"I can help."

"You?" He was surprised by the anger in her eyes as Margaret looked at him. "Don't tell me running a trucking empire gave you enough leisure to take a course in midwifery as well?"

"Nothing so interesting," Matt said calmly. "I went to Lamaze classes with my sister, Susan, because her army husband was away on active duty."

Seeing the nurse come out, Margaret said, "I have to go back in."

"I've told her to rest for a while," the nurse said. "Why don't you get something to eat, before you go back in there? I'll watch her on the television monitor in the nurse's station."

Margaret glanced at the room uncertainly. "I don't want to leave her."

"She'll be fine," Matt assured her. "And after we eat, I'll come in with you."

"Both of you can be with her now, but later the doctor's going to allow only one of you in the delivery room," the nurse warned. "Decide who it's going to be, and I'll leave gown, cap and mask out for you. You'll have to scrub up when we move her into the birthing room."

Margaret stiffened as she felt an arm go around her shoulders and heard the chuckle in Matt's voice as he said, "I know how much you want to be in there, Margaret. Stop looking so worried. We'll toss a coin for the privilege after we eat."

He seemed to know his way around because he steered her directly to the hospital cafeteria. Margaret was beginning to have a suspicion the man knew his way around everything and everyone.

"The special is roast beef on rye," Matt said looking at the board on the wall. "The alternatives are fish and chips, chicken cordon bleu or turkey and all the trimmings."

Margaret hadn't eaten since morning, but she wasn't hungry. Picking up a carton of chocolate milk, she said, "This is all I want right now."

"You'll feel better if you eat something," Matt said, with a frown.

"I'll eat later." When it was all over. When she knew for sure she wasn't going to make a fool of herself by throwing up or fainting.

Picking up a glass, Margaret headed for the cash register. The customer in front of her opened her bag to pay, reminding Margaret she had no purse with her, therefore no money. Panicked, she turned to look at Matt. "I don't have any money."

"I have enough for both of us."

For both of us. The way the phrase linked them together disturbed Margaret.

"Ring it up together, please," she heard him say as she stared blankly ahead, trying to smother the emotions tumbling inside her.

Spotting an empty table by the window, Margaret hurried over to it, trying to figure out the compelling need to get as much distance between herself and Matthew Magnum as she could.

"Margaret, hi!"

She looked up to see Joe Graines. In his long lab technician's coat, he looked very different from the Joe who in high school had traded repair work on Beelzebub, for book reports. "Joe! How nice to see you. Won't you join us?"

It was the perfect solution. Joe's easygoing ways would definitely defuse any tension, real or imaginary, between her and Matthew Magnum.

A prickle at the back of her neck warned Margaret Matt was close by. "Mr. Magnum and I had to give someone a ride into the hospital. She's in labor."

"Hi, Matt!" Joe waited until Matt placed his tray on the table and, then the two men shook hands. "The person you brought in wouldn't happen to be Gina?"

Surprised, Margaret asked, "You know Gina?"

"Gina and Jack rent the upstairs apartment from me, but I'm going to move there, and let them have the downstairs now the baby's here." Joe stood up. "I think I'll run up and keep her company for a while, so don't hurry with your meal.''

Margaret smiled. "Thanks, Joe."

"Anything for you, Margaret," he said good-naturedly. "See you around Matt."

"Known Joe long?" Matt asked as he reached for the salt, puzzled by the interest he felt in her answer.

"All my life," Margaret said. "We went to school together.''

"Any romance between you two?"

"I beg your pardon?" She set her glass down with a small thud.

"You know the story line," he said patiently. "High school sweethearts reunited. Passion blazes.''

"That's none of your business," Margaret snapped.

"I just wondered what keeps Joe in Inchwater.''

Margaret immediately jumped to Joe's defence. "Joe's a wonderful person. He's easygoing, always ready to fix everyone's car, always ready to lend a helping hand. Just because he's content to live in Inchwater doesn't mean he's a failure.''

Matt reached across the table and laid a hand on hers. Margaret snatched hers away.

"Margaret, stop fluffing your feathers as if I'm attacking one of your chicks. I like Joe Graines.''

"You do?"

"What makes you think I'd feel anyone who chose to live in Inchwater is a failure? Success isn't making a million, or being approved of by the world. It's self-approval and contentment. Joe's at peace with the world because he has both these qualities. Too many people have to pay a therapist to teach them how to handle life.''

"Oh!" Matt's words took the wind out of Margaret's sails. After a moment, a thought occurred to Margaret. "Why are we having this conversation about Joe?"

Matt looked at her. The urge to make her aware that she had a life of her own to live was stronger than ever. For Tim's sake, he assured himself, refusing to think about other, deeper reasons. It was time for part two of his plan.

"I just wanted to know I'm not stepping on anyone's toes."

"Doing what?" She raised her glass to her mouth, wanting to hide from the intensity in his gaze.

"Courting you."

Margaret choked, coughed and spluttered, as the chocolate milk went down the wrong way. "Excuse me?"

Matt chewed, swallowed and then stated very calmly, "You're an old-fashioned girl, Margaret, and so I've decided to court you the old-fashioned way."

"Co-co-co..." she coughed again.

"Drink some water," he said kindly. "Yes, Margaret. My first impression of you was wrong. I don't think an affair will suit you so I've decided to court you." His eyes, alight with laughter, belied his serious expression.

He was making fun of her again. Teasing her. Margaret's temper blazed. "Why you male chauvinist..."

"*Paging Ms. Browning. Paging Margaret Browning. Please return to Maternity.*"

The well-modulated voice cut through the red fog of her anger. Margaret reached the door before she realized he was at her elbow.

"You don't have to come," she flung at him. "Finish your meal."

"I can eat later," he said, matching her pace. "I told you, I've had training in Lamaze. I can help."

"Gina's water broke, and she's getting nervous," the nurse informed them, meeting them at the door of the room. "We have two women about to deliver at any time, and the nursing shortage means I can't spare anyone to stay with her all the time. That's why I paged you...."

"Thanks," Margaret said.

"Nurse, I went to Lamaze classes with my sister last year. If I could . . ." The voices faded as Margaret entered the room and shut the door behind her.

Joe stood up, his face awash with relief. "Margaret's here."

Another scared soul? Margaret wondered.

Gina turned frightened eyes on her. "My water broke, but the nurse says it's still going to be about two hours from now."

"You're lucky," Margaret said, picking up a damp washcloth and smoothing it over Gina's face and neck, with a hand that shook slightly. "An article I read recently stated most first-time mothers are in labor for longer periods."

"I'll see you later, ladies. Don't have too much fun. If it wasn't for the call of duty, I would love to stay." Joe retreated hurriedly.

Margaret fluffed up Gina's pillows and smiled. "You're doing fine."

"Gina, did I ever tell you about the time my sister, Susan, found out she was pregnant?" Confidently Matt entered the room and took control of the situation, positioning himself on the other side of Gina's bed. He picked up the girl's hand, and Margaret had to admit touching came as naturally to the man as breathing. Admit, too, that some of the tension left her because he was there.

"No."

He smiled, and nothing could disguise the male vitality he oozed. The cleft in his chin should be cited a hazard. Margaret shook her head slightly to throw off the ridiculous impressions her mind registered.

"Pete, my brother-in-law, had just been stationed abroad when Susan found out she was pregnant. She called Pete up right away, and told him he had to come home at once. There was no way she could have this baby on her own. When Pete told her he couldn't because he was an active duty, Susan sat down and wrote a five-page letter to his commanding officer, telling him what she thought of rules that kept couples apart at times like this. If he couldn't send Pete home on *paternity* leave, she concluded, she was coming there to have this baby.''

Gina burst out laughing. Matt smiled, and Margaret had to force her gaze away from the deep cleft in his chin again. ''She finally got used to being pregnant,'' he said solemnly, ''but it took her the complete nine months. Luckily for Susan, Patricia, my other sister, and myself, Pete arrived a month before the baby was born.''

''Ooh!'' Gina doubled over, and before Margaret could move, Matthew had an arm around her shoulders. ''Easy now. Little breaths. One, two, three, four. That's it. Now again. One, two, three, four. You're doing great.''

His gaze was fixed on her, and Margaret had the strangest sensation the last words were meant for her, as well.

Feeling as limp as the washcloth in her hand, she wiped the sweat from Gina's face. The last contraction had been a big one. How much longer could this go on?

A bustle at the door proved to be the arrival of the nurse. ''I need to be alone with Gina for a few minutes,'' she said.

''We'll be right outside.''

Margaret stalked to the door ahead of Matthew. When she heard it close, she turned on him. ''Jack would have been here if he wasn't a trucker.''

''Hey!'' Two hands came down to cup her shoulders. ''I know this is rough and scary, but that's no reason to hit below the belt. There are a great many men whose jobs prevent them from being with their wives at important times. What about those in the armed forces?''

''Jack should have been here,'' Margaret repeated stubbornly. ''He's not defending our country or human rights, he's just driving a stupid truck somewhere." It was all back . . . the old pain and bitterness. The time her parents hadn't been home when she'd fallen and had to have three stitches in her knee, the night she'd burned up with a high fever and wanted them to hold her. Sometimes her mother had been home but she'd gone with her father whenever she could.

The pressure on Margaret's shoulders increased slightly, forcing her mind back to the present. "Do you think Gina would rather have a husband beside her with no job and no money, or one who's able to provide for her and the baby, but who can't always be with her?"

He was right of course. As usual. Unable to say anything more, Margaret simply leaned against the wall. She was going to save her strength for what was yet to come. The back of her top was damp, and her knees felt as if someone had replaced them with cotton wool. Closing her eyes, she forced herself to take deep breaths, conjure up a calm scene. All she could see was Gina's face contracted with pain.

"So much fire," Matt said. "I wonder if it's only in your hair."

Her eyes flew open to see him rubbing a lock of her hair between thumb and forefinger.

As their gazes meshed, Matt felt the electricity between them. The panic in Margaret's eyes told Matt she was aware of it, too. She might not want it, but it was definitely there. He looked at her mouth, and Margaret's lips parted slightly.

"You try to appear as if you're always in control, don't you Margaret?" Matt asked. "But your eyes and hair give you away. The former tells me your sophisticated air is not even skin-deep, and your hair hints at hidden fires within you."

He watched the confusion in her eyes deepen.

The door opened and the nurse said, "You can go in now. She's doing fine."

Matt moved away, wondering about the attraction he felt towards Margaret Browning. She was all wrong for him. She had shown very clearly that she wanted nothing to do with truckers and trucking. To let himself become involved with someone like her was as smart as touching a plugged-in iron to see if it was hot.

"Mr. Magnum!"

Margaret turned to see a husky young man hurry down the hospital corridor to them and cling to the strong hand outstretched toward him. "How is Gina?"

Margaret stared at the newcomer. This must be Gina's husband. Where had he come from?

"Fine . . . see for yourself." Matt pushed open the door of the room behind them.

Jack went through the door as the nurse asked, "The husband?"

Matthew Magnum nodded. "Yes."

They heard Gina say, "Jack! Oh, Jack!"

"Baby, are you all right?" There was no mistaking the love in her husband's hoarse voice.

Matthew Magnum shut the door gently, giving the couple the privacy they needed.

The nurse beamed at him. "Now, which fairy godmother managed that? We love happy endings here at Garrison Community."

As the woman walked away, Margaret asked, "How did he get here?"

She continued to prop herself up against the wall, unable to believe the suddenness with which she had been relieved of her task.

"I called the truck stop, and the men contacted him on the CB. I'm not sure yet, but I guess another trucker must have offered to give him a ride back here. I hope you're not too disappointed that your help is no longer necessary?"

She glared at Matt, ignoring the teasing light in his eyes. "What about Jack's truck?"

"Parked somewhere safely till another driver can get to it."

"What about his driving schedule? Won't he get behind and lose money if he doesn't make his delivery on time?" In her father's time, a man had been fired for being too ill to go into work.

"Why the sudden change of heart?" His smile told Margaret that Matt wasn't angry, simply curious.

Margaret wet her lips. "I may not like the fact Jack is a trucker, but I'm concerned about him as a person. He can't lose his new job now, with a baby to support."

"Stop worrying, Margaret. Jack won't suffer in any way. If any questions are asked, they'll be asked of Bedouin Trucking, not the drivers. My guess is that one of my men had already taken over and will get the job done for Jack."

"How?"

"He'll hitch a ride with another trucker going in that direction, pick up Jack's truck and complete the run."

"You don't mind that he left his truck just like that?"

"Why should I? It isn't every day a man can be present at the birth of his child. This baby's birth is going to make news waves over the CB radio before the night is over. We truckers stick together. I bet right now there are a great many good wishes being sent over the air for Jack and Gina."

"Oh."

It was a whole new concept. And had he said "we truckers"? Margaret shook her head. Her thoughts were all bouncing around in her head again, confusing her. It would take a while to sort them out.

"What made you decide to call it Bedouin Trucking?" Margaret asked.

She was unprepared for the way Matthew Magnum's eyes darkened. "I named my company after a man who made a very big difference in my life."

Margaret nodded, aware he didn't want to discuss the subject further.

"What do you plan to do now that our services are no longer required?" he asked after a small pause.

Margaret checked he wristwatch. It was barely four o'clock. If the nurse's predictions were right, the baby wouldn't be born before six o'clock. She intended to stay around until then. "I'm going upstairs to visit a friend of mine who works in administration," Margaret said. "Helen Swatchey and I went to school together. Don't wait for me. I'll get a ride home with Joe."

"Right." His nod indicated perfect compliance with her plans.

On the elevator going up, Margaret tried to puzzle Matthew Magnum out. She had seen so many different facets of the man today. Humor, as he'd teased her and told the story of his sister, gentleness, as he'd helped Gina through her pain, understanding her fears. Underlying it all was Matt's demand that she take a closer look at her own needs, reach out to life before it was too late. Margaret took a deep breath. Matthew Magnum was like a strong current, and she felt herself helplessly tugged along by him.

The elevator door opened and Margaret stared blankly out at the corridor for a second before she realized this was the floor the offices were on. Collecting her rampaging thoughts she headed for the room where her friend worked.

An hour and a half later, Margaret entered the waiting room and stopped short. Matthew Magnum rose from the couch where he'd been sitting, his head propped up against the wall, his long legs stretched out in front of him. "There you are," he said as if she had asked him to wait for her.

"Yes," Margaret snapped, angered by the thrill of excitement that coursed down her spine at the sight of him. "How's Gina?"

"It's all over, earlier than anticipated. A baby girl. Gina's in Room 110."

Margaret turned away. "I'll go in and see her."

A hand on her shoulder stopped her. "Not in this mood. What's happened? You look like a thundercloud."

"Nothing." Margaret held herself stiffly, wishing she could grow horns on her shoulders to butt his hand away. "Why are you still here?"

Matt wondered why she was always so tense around him.

"I'm waiting for you," he said easily. "Joe's working a double shift, so you won't be able to ride back with him till tomorrow morning."

"I'll find my own way home," she snapped.

Matt wondered how long it had been since Margaret had allowed anyone to take care of her.

"Go see Gina. Maybe you'll feel better after that." Matt turned her toward the door and let her go.

Margaret knocked, before entering Gina's room. Gina looked exhausted, but her eyes shone with happiness. Jack sat beside her on the bed, his shoulder supporting his wife, beaming with pride.

"Congratulations, you two."

"Margaret, this, as you know, is Jack, my husband. Jack this is Janet's niece, Margaret, whom I told you about," Gina said with all the impatience of a new mother, hurrying through what wasn't really important to what was. "Have you seen Mikela Margaret?"

"Not yet," Margaret said, leaning forward to kiss Gina, surprised they liked her name enough to use it as the baby's middle name.

"She's perfect," Jack announced proudly. "Six pounds, three ounces. Thank you for staying with Gina."

"I didn't do a thing," Margaret protested. "In fact, I think I was more nervous than Gina."

"I know you were." Gina smiled. "But you did help me. The fact that you were scared but still determined to be with me, made me feel really good. I was more afraid of being alone than of the pain."

Jack said hesitantly, "We'd like you and Mr. Magnum to be godparents, if you don't mind."

"It would be a privilege," Margaret said quickly, wondering if she could insert a clause into the new contract she had just accepted.

She would gladly be the baby's godmother as long as her duties didn't include having anything to do with Matthew Magnum.

They chatted for ten minutes before Margaret left. Outside the nursery, she paused and examined the cribs through the glass. The new babies' cribs were lined up by the window. Four boys and one girl. Mikela Margaret had the place of honor in the center, in a pink crib. Margaret stared at the downy soft skin, the dark crinkled hair and the perfectly beautiful jet black eyes, and her throat closed up. She sniffed.

"Quite something, isn't it?" a voice said close behind her.

"What?" Why was Matthew Magnum calling the most darling baby in the world *it?*

"The beauty of creation."

She spun toward him, her mouth rounded in a perfect O of surprise, amazed by his apt choice of words. As their gazes meshed, she became aware of tension gathering in the pit of her stomach. The look in Matt's eyes glinted with the same awareness. In the space of a few seconds they had become a man and a woman with an undeniable chemistry pulsing between them.

A hand came up to cup her cheek, an unspoken message flashed between them and then he bent forward and kissed her. Casually, lightly, *sweetly.*

"Congratulations, godmother," Margaret heard him say softly, the wicked glint back in his eyes. "Let's leave before the hospital thinks we're permanent fixtures here and puts us on the payroll. I hear they have vacancies in Maternity, a spot after your own heart."

She searched for words to annihilate the man with, to tell him she wasn't taken in by his humor at all, or his casual kisses, but her vocal chords seemed paralyzed. The only clear memory imprinted on her brain was of a warm, firm mouth on hers, the momentary mingling of their breaths and the fact that in that instant she had leaned toward Matthew Magnum.

For more.

Chapter Five

He couldn't believe he had kissed her, Matt told himself, as he worked late into the night. True, it was just a light, friendly kiss, but it hadn't been part of the plan. Matt tried to analyze why he felt the way he did and drew a blank.

Shrugging it off as a whim brought on by the circumstances surrounding the birth of the baby, he tried to concentrate on his computer monitor.

Margaret came out of her room just as Timmy came out of his the next morning.

"Hi!" Margaret said, noticing the tiny shaving cut on her brother's cheek. His hair, wet from the shower, looked darker than hers and he seemed as if he had grown another inch in the night.

"Morning." Timmy's brown eyes, so like her own, reflected none of her own cheer.

Margaret smiled. Aunt Jan and she were morning people. Timmy definitely wasn't.

"How was work yesterday?" Margaret asked as they went downstairs.

"Okay."

"Would you like to go shopping today after work?" Margaret ignored the cautious note in Timmy's voice. She had noticed that Timmy's jeans looked threadbare and his shirts exposed his thin wrists. "We could shop in the new mall in Garrison, maybe even stop off for a movie and a bite to eat."

"Can't. Mr. Magnum's going to show me how to change a tire on a truck tonight. See you later, sis."

He was gone before Margaret could ask him about breakfast. She stared after him blankly as a frisson of fear snaked through her stomach. What was happening to them? Timmy had barely glanced at her.

Going into the kitchen Margaret decided not to worry Aunt Jan with Timmy's strange behavior. Very soon she would have to have a serious talk with Timmy, make him understand why she was so afraid about his new job.

Winning him over wouldn't be easy, Margaret knew. Not while Matthew Magnum was so firmly on Timmy's side. On her way to the hospital to visit Gina that evening, Margaret thought of everything that had happened since the first day of her vacation. She had to find some way of getting through to Timmy, in spite of Matthew Magnum.

Gina was surprised to see Margaret. "You didn't have to come," she protested.

"I wanted to," Margaret said. "Besides, the only alternative I had to visiting you was doing some weeding and I'd rather do that early in the day."

Jack had stopped by The Inner Man that morning and told Aunt Jan and Margaret that Gina wouldn't be coming home today as planned. For some reason, Gina's blood pressure was on the high side, and Dr. Reddy had decided to keep her in over the weekend.

"How do you like working in the restaurant?" Gina asked Margaret, smiling at her daughter who nursed vigorously at her breast.

"Aunt Jan hired two new people yesterday, so I'm out of a job again," Margaret said lightly. "Both of the women are truckers' wives. It seems Matt sent them. I helped her with an inventory of the dishes today, but I think she just gave me that job to make me feel needed. How have you been doing? Are you looking forward to going home?"

A smile lit Gina's face as she nodded. "Do you know Joe's letting us have the downstairs apartment? Wasn't that thoughtful of him? Said it would be safer for the baby, and less of a strain on me."

"And Mr. Magnum's wonderful, too. He got Jack back for me and Mikki," Gina reflected.

"Where's Jack?" Margaret asked quickly.

If Inchwater had a town square, she wouldn't be surprised to see a statue of Matthew Magnum put up there by the inhabitants. She would be the only one who wouldn't contribute to it.

Oh, wouldn't you?

Margaret felt the color rise in her face as she recalled the feel of Matt's mouth on hers, the way he'd understood her fears in the labor ward yesterday.

A small frown of worry crossed Gina's face. "Jack stopped by earlier for a little while. He's making a run to Las Vegas this evening and from there, he's going to Phoenix. It's for the man who took over his run. He'll be back the day after tomorrow, and then he starts his vacation. He's cleaned out the apartment and moved all our things downstairs." Regret flickered in Gina's eyes. "I meant to have everything so nice before Mikki arrived, but it didn't work out that way. I even had paint for her room picked out at Jensen's Hardware."

Margaret took Mikki from Gina and patted the baby's back to burp her. As she cuddled the infant, an idea came to her. She could paint Mikki's room. It would be her gift to the baby.

"Jack's been talking to one of the drivers who's been with Bedouin Trucking since it started," said Gina. "Did you know that our Mr. Magnum is a millionaire? Who'd have thought he was so important? I mean, he doesn't lord it over the rest of us, or anything."

"I didn't know he was so rich," Margaret said. "The trucking business must pay very well."

Gina shook her head. "It isn't only that. He inherited money from his father. The family owns a shipping business."

A half hour later, Margaret stood up. "I have to leave now. Beelzebub's acting up again, and I came in on the bus."

"How will you get back?"

"The same way I got here. The bus." A regular bus service from Barstow to Las Vegas stopped at Garrison and Inchwater. "I'll see you tomorrow."

Her thoughts were on her conversation with Gina. It was hard to imagine Matthew Magnum as a millionaire. She thought of the jeans and checked shirts he wore. His clothes, his manner, even his worn-out wallet, all attested to an ordinary man.

"Hello, Margaret!"

She jumped and looked straight into a pair of mocking green eyes. The fact that he had appeared as she was thinking about him was the only reason, Margaret told herself, for the confusion flooding her.

"Hi." Matt held a huge potted plant and had apparently been waiting for the elevator she had just got out from.

"Do you have a minute?" he asked, turning away from the elevator and falling into step beside her.

"What is it?" asked Margaret reluctantly.

"Janet mentioned you have nothing to do in the restaurant now that she's hired two new employees. I need someone to help me with filing and light bookkeeping. Would you be interested in a temporary job?"

Margaret came to a halt and turned to look at Matt. "You're not serious."

"I am. You work during the summers and I have a vacancy in the office."

Margaret wondered why Matthew Magnum had such a hard time accepting her aversion to trucking. "Maybe you haven't realized, but I want nothing to do with trucking, nothing at all," she said clearly.

"It would give you a chance to see what goes on first hand," he persisted. "You'll soon realize there's nothing to be afraid of."

Margaret lifted her chin. "I won't work for you and I'm not going to change my mind about trucking," she said through clenched teeth.

Matt looked at her and then shrugged. "Thought I'd give it a try for Janet and Timmy's sake."

He walked away, leaving Margaret feeling like a three-year-old who had just thrown an unreasonable tantrum. Biting her lower lip in anger she walked out of the hospital lobby. Every time she ran into Matthew Magnum he reduced her to this level. Confused, angry, *disturbed*.

While he waited for the elevator, Matt realized he hadn't handled that very well. The band around his chest told him there was more to his offering Margaret Browning a job than the desire to help Timmy or Janet. For some reason he had felt she would jump at it, and she hadn't. He hadn't been left in any doubt about her reasons, either.

He had hoped she would take up the job. It would have been easier to wear away her objections to Timmy's working around trucks on a daily basis. Now he would have to think of something else.

It wasn't going to be easy to make Margaret see why she had to let go of Timmy and lead her own life. Stubbornness had to be added to the list he'd made of her qualities. Good, old-fashioned traits like honesty and saying what was on her mind headed the list. In Inchwater these traits might not be considered uncommon but in the world Matt had grown up in, these qualities were almost extinct. To Matt they set Margaret apart from all the other women he had ever known.

Matt's mouth tightened as he thought of that aspect of his life. The determination never to follow in his father's footsteps wasn't limited to the work his father had done, or his life-style. It extended to women as well. Matt had never understood why his shrewd, tough father had let the women in his life walk all over him. Once Maximilian Magnum had told Matt it was the only way to keep them happy, but it had never worked for him. Each time a relationship disintegrated his father had been devastated, yet it had never taught him caution of any kind or prevented him from plunging into another relationship as soon as possible. Only Matt and his sisters knew about their father's depressions, and the long stays at the clinic in Switzerland, while everyone thought he was vacationing in the French Riviera.

A man came and stood beside Matt, holding a teddy bear and some books. He looked at Matt's plant and smiled. Matt nodded politely, and went back to his thoughts.

A long time ago Matt had decided no woman was going to control him. He would never give anyone the power that accompanied trust and love.

"Going up?"

Matt looked at the elevator filled with people, watching him curiously as they held the door open for him. "Yes, thanks."

He stepped into it and stared at the smooth, shiny surface of the doors as they closed. No woman, with the exception of his sisters, had ever gotten close to him. And none ever would, he swore silently.

Jensen's Hardware was only three blocks away from the hospital, and Margaret was there in ten minutes. Frank Jensen, the owner and a close friend of Aunt Jan's, was delighted to see her. They talked about Washington and Margaret's work for a while. Business, Mr. Jensen told her, was booming, and of course he remembered the shade of paint Gina Wade had picked out. He had written the color down for her. Misty lavender. Margaret asked for a two-gallon can to be mixed while she picked out sandpaper, rollers and other odds and ends.

She was in one of the aisles when she heard Mr. Jensen say, "Good evening, Mr. Magnum. Can I help you?"

Retreating to the rear of the store so he wouldn't see her was a reflex action. Margaret stared at a line of bathroom fixtures blankly. Why couldn't she even turn around without running into Matthew Magnum? She hadn't recovered from the encounter at the hospital and here he was again.

"Margaret!" Mr. Jensen called loudly from the next aisle a few minutes later. "Margaret, where are you? Mr. Magnum has offered to give you a ride home. It will save carrying that heavy paint on the bus."

She came forward reluctantly. "There's no need for that. I still have a few things to pick out, and I don't want to keep Mr. Magnum waiting."

"Waiting is one of the things I do best," Matt told her with an easy smile. "I'm here to pick up some supplies for the truck stop. I'll drive you home when you're ready. Going to paint the restaurant?"

Matt could tell she didn't want him waiting for her or offering her a ride home. Margaret's independence wrapped her like a coat of quills on a porcupine.

"She's painting the baby's room for Gina and Jack Wade," Mr. Jensen told him. "Gina's kind of disappointed she couldn't have the baby's room ready, and Jack is off on a two-day trip to Phoenix."

Garrison didn't need a newspaper, Margaret thought, while it had Mr. Jensen. Did he have to go and tell Matthew Magnum everything?

"Mikki's room?" Matt asked, noticing Margaret's annoyance.

The fact she didn't want anything to do with him had to be responsible for the idea that popped into his mind. This could be a way of getting to know her.

She nodded reluctantly. Matt looked at the supplies lined up on the counter and said, "How about one of those wallpaper borders? They are easy to put up and make a real difference to a plain wall."

Matt interpreted Margaret's mind-your-own-business expression correctly. It was hard to keep from smiling.

Mr. Jensen beamed. "Excellent idea. They're the latest in wall designs. You'll find them by the far wall, Margaret.

"As we're going to paint the room together, I'll help you pick out the border," Matt said easily.

"To-to-together?" stammered Margaret.

He nodded firmly. "I have a vested interest in Mikki. She's my goddaughter, too."

"I don't need help," Margaret said abruptly. "And I don't want a border."

Mr. Jensen looked shocked at her rudeness, but Matt only smiled. "I do."

He walked over to the wall and looked at the rolls there. "We have to be careful about what we pick out. Susan tells me the latest research on children claims babies *do* notice their surroundings. What do you think of scarlet poppies? Might inspire Mikki to be a painter. Or this one? Geometric patterns? I have never agreed with the view that women don't have a head for math." He heard the exasperated sigh that escaped Margaret as she walked over and joined him by the wall display. "A border of musical notes? Mikki could grow up playing the violin in the Philharmonic, thanks to us."

This close, Margaret could see the teasing laughter in Matt's eyes. The scent of pines wrapped her, and she turned away quickly as her heart picked up its pace. Overwhelmed by his nearness, she reached up blindly for a border, and heard him say. "Pumpkins? I don't think so."

His laughter stirred her hair. Angry with the effect he was having on her, Margaret turned to him. "I don't want your help, Mr. Magnum," she said bluntly. "You can't charm your way into my life, as you have done with everybody else. I won't let you. Timmy might think the world of you but I don't, and the less we have to do with each other, the better."

She saw the snap of anger in his eyes before it vanished. "What has painting a room got to do with your brother?" asked Matt. "Or is this another instance of how you can't separate anything in your life from his?"

Margaret swallowed to get rid of the lump of anger in her throat before she could speak. "Your comments aren't going to stop me from trying to make him change his mind about his present job. I'm getting tired of your personal attacks on me."

In the silence that followed Margaret heard Mr. Jensen discussing exterior paint with a customer in another aisle.

"Unlike you, I would not use any influence I might have with your brother to force him into a career he doesn't want," Matt said.

"I want what's best for Timmy," Margaret said stubbornly.

"Then untie those emotional apron strings and let him make his own decision."

Margaret looked at Matthew Magnum's face and felt like hurling a can of paint at his head. An *open* can of paint.

"Have you found something you like?"

Margaret looked at Mr. Jensen's smiling face and shook her head. "Not yet." She couldn't continue the argument with Matt in front of the store owner. Besides, she had nothing more to say right now.

Determined to concentrate on the task at hand, Margaret looked at the borders carefully, finally picking out one that had purple teddy bears with enormous pink bows on a cream background.

"Mikki's going to like that," Matt said behind her. "I won't be long. I just have to get another paint roller and a couple more things."

"There's a new spray gun that does the work in half the time," Mr. Jensen suggested.

Matt shook his head. "That won't do. Margaret likes doing things the old-fashioned way."

Margaret felt warmth surge to her face. Matthew Magnum gave the impression he knew her well. His casual familiarity was intensely disturbing.

"The new paint you've bought is excellent," Mr. Jensen said. "All you have to do is clean the wall and apply it. One coat is usually all you need."

Margaret kept quiet as the purchases were totalled. As Magnum took his wallet out of his hip pocket, she said fiercely, "I'm going to pay the bill."

He turned to her and said mockingly, "Margaret, didn't anyone teach you about sharing a godchild? I'll pay for half the supplies."

Margaret extracted her share of the money silently from her bag. Painting Mikki's room was no longer going to be the calm, peaceful task she had envisioned.

"Good night!" Mr. Jensen called as they left the store. "Enjoy your painting."

"So, when do we start?" Matt asked a few minutes later, as his car covered the miles to Inchwater.

Margaret swallowed. "You aren't serious about wanting to help are you?" Her voice held surprise mixed with resignation.

"One hundred percent," he said firmly.

"Painting is hard work," Margaret warned.

"I know." He nodded. "Scraping, sanding, primer, base coat, top coat, trim. I painted a house one summer," Matt continued. "So, when do we start?"

"Tonight," Margaret said reluctantly. "I thought around eight. Aunt Jan's favorite detective show comes on then, and she goes to bed after that."

The car stopped in front of the restaurant, and Matthew Magnum nodded. "Eight o'clock at Joe's. It's a date."

Margaret hurried out.

It's a date.

It was just a casual expression, Margaret told herself sternly, but she couldn't stop the tremors of excitement that coursed through her.

Janet looked up from the magazine she was reading on the garden swing as Margaret entered the backyard. "How are Gina and Mikki doing?"

"They're both fine," Margaret said absently. "I'm going to paint Mikki's room, as a surprise for them. Jack's going to be away for two days. If I start tonight I can have it all done before he gets back. Where's Timmy?"

"He's at T.J.'s watching a video." T.J.'s parents owned Inchwater's only grocery store and lived behind it.

Margaret hesitated and then asked, "Is it my imagination, or is Timmy avoiding me?"

"I think," said Aunt Jan, "that he's simply trying to avoid a confrontation. He knows you don't approve of his job, and rather than argue with you about it, he prefers to stay out of the way. Give him time. He'll come around."

Margaret sat on the swing beside Aunt Jan. Images of Timmy and herself as children flashed into her mind. Had she really driven the brother she loved so dearly away?

"Aunt Jan, do you think I'm wrong in not wanting Timmy to be a trucker?"

"He hasn't said he wants to be one yet, has he?" Aunt Jan pointed out in her usual calm manner. "Don't worry about something that might never happen. Did you find someone to give you a ride home?"

Deciding not to worry Aunt Jan by arguing about Timmy and trucking, Margaret got to her feet. "I'm going to call Joe and ask him to drop off a spare key to Gina's place on his way to work."

There had to be a way to heal things between her and Timmy. He had to realize she was on his side, that she wanted nothing but the best for him. She couldn't run the risk of losing him. Margaret was halfway up the stairs before she realized she hadn't answered Aunt Jan's last question.

As for Matthew Magnum's accusation that she couldn't separate her life from Timmy's, she didn't have to prove anything to him.

Matt leaned against the aluminum siding of Joe's house, watching Margaret approach. The old shirt she wore almost covered her shorts. Her hair was tied back and she wore sneakers. Her long, lovely legs stopped when she saw him. Matt quickly looked away from them to her face.

Margaret's mouth twisted at the sight of Matthew Magnum in blue work overalls and a blue-and-white checked shirt. The cap on his head, turned front to back, made it look as if he were auditioning for the role of painter.

"Ready to work?" he asked.

"Ready to work," she agreed.

Opening the front door with the key Joe had given her, Margaret switched the lights on and went directly to what was going to be the baby's room. Her mouth fell open as she looked around. The walls had been scraped clean of the old paint. Whirling, she looked at Matt.

"I had the afternoon free, so I hope you don't mind that I got started," Matt said casually. "Joe gave me Jack's spare key to the place."

He had made time, so he could get this part of the work done.

The supplies sat on an old table in the middle of the floor, which was covered with newspaper. A small transistor radio provided soft classical tunes. The baseboard had been taped over with masking tape. Matthew Magnum, Margaret could see, had been very busy.

He opened the can of paint and stirred it before pouring it into a tray. "Pretty color. Wish they had a rose exactly this shade."

Determined to be very businesslike, Margaret picked up a roller and dipped it into the paint. "I'll do these two walls, you do the others."

"Yes, ma'am." The teasing rejoinder drew a dark glance. During her first year as a teacher, Margaret's class had consisted of thirty unruly ten-year-olds. Walking over here, she had told herself, that if she could control children she could certainly quell Matt's irrepressible humor.

They worked in silence for a while, and then he said, "The paint will dry overnight if we leave the window open."

Margaret nodded. "I'll come back tomorrow afternoon to fix the border and finish the trim."

"That's my border," he reminded her. "You didn't want to buy it, remember? *I'll* fix it."

Margaret bit down on her lower lip. He really was the most aggravating man she knew. "Very well," she said stiffly.

Working in here this afternoon, Matt had thought of their argument in the paint store and come up with the first step of his plan. Margaret had to let go of her brother before she destroyed both the trust and the love that made them so close.

"Tim is a great kid, Margaret," he said carefully. "He can take care of himself. He's intelligent enough to make the right decisions about his future."

The silence made him look at her over his shoulder. She had stopped painting, but still faced the wall.

"It's time you start concentrating on yourself," he added.

Margaret turned, and Matt saw the anger on her face. "I did not come here for a lecture on my life-style," she said furiously.

"Don't make Tim your excuse for avoiding life, Margaret," Matt continued, as if she hadn't spoken. "There's more to living than watching out for your brother."

Margaret glared at him as the last vestige of her self-control shattered.

"I know exactly what is behind all this," she bit out. "You can't believe my refusal to join the Matthew Magnum fan club. Is the offer to join me in the painting another attempt at bowling me over? Well let me tell you, Mr. Magnum, that no matter how long you stay in Inchwater, my attitude toward you isn't going to change."

Matt held her gaze steadily. "Is that what you really think, Margaret? That my main purpose in staying here is to bowl you over?"

Taking the roller from her nerveless fingers, he set it next to his own in the painting tray and straightened. Margaret took a step away from him.

"If you back up any farther, you're going to stick to the wall," Matt said casually. "I want to talk to you not pounce on you, so relax. Let's set some things straight, for the record. For one thing, I never intentionally set out to

bowl anyone over. Premeditated romance is too cold for
me. For another I said what I did because I care about you
and Timmy the way any decent human being cares about
another. I would have thought growing up in Inchwater,
where values still mean something, you could understand
that. I don't want you to shelve your happiness for Timmy's. I see the way you ride herd on him. You're going to
get hurt when he jerks out of your grasp if you don't let go
on your own."

Their gazes meshed and silence wrapped them for a
minute before he said, "I am not staying in Inchwater to
lure you into my bed, Margaret. I was just joking when I
made the remark the other day. I'm here because Bedouin
Trucking has been having problems."

"Wh—what kind of problems?" Margaret decided she
might as well know the whole of it, before she found a
stone to crawl under.

"On arrival, losses have been discovered in some of the
shipments we carry. One box of electronic equipment, another of medicines. Nothing large enough to require a police complaint, but it concerns me. Other trucking
companies haven't reported losses. Bedouin Trucking has
always had an unimpeachable reputation, and I am determined to get to the bottom of it before it gets worse."

"Oh," Margaret said, feeling very small.

At a lost for words, she picked up her roller and went
back to work. Nothing she said would make things better,
and she certainly didn't want to make them any worse.

*I care about you and Timmy the way any decent human
being cares about another.*

He had certainly made the basis of their relationship
very clear. General, distant, *formal*.

Margaret's hand moved back and forth in quick strokes.
The storm had really cleared the air, but why was she left
with this sensation of chaos? Her thoughts kept her so
busy, Margaret didn't realize how late it was until she came

to the end of her second wall. Turning around she watched Matt at work, the muscles of his back bunched under his shirt. The width of his shoulders and the strength of his arms produced an odd sensation in her throat.

A little later, he stopped and turned. Margaret looked away quickly, wishing it hadn't been so obvious she had been staring at him.

Matt said, "Done in record time. This calls for a celebration."

"A celebration?"

He nodded. "I have a frozen pizza in the fridge. Do you like anchovies?"

"Not really," Margaret answered cautiously.

"Neither do I," he said cheerfully. "I got a cheese pizza because it's going to be a while before I get to know all your preferences. I'll put it in the oven and be right back."

He left the room and Margaret stared after him.

It's going to be a while before I get to know your preferences. Matt had sounded as if they were definitely going to get to know each other better. Margaret looked around the room. It would never do to let him see the way he got to her. The walls looked very pretty. She looked at the naked bulb hanging from the ceiling and frowned. It needed a shade of some sort to soften its glare.

"We make a good team," Matt commented, bending to spread a small, disposable tablecloth on top of the newspaper before setting paper cups and plates on it.

A team, as in two people on the same side? Margaret swallowed.

Matt opened an ice chest and took out sodas and a salad.

"I really should be getting home," Margaret said. A voice over the radio station had just announced it was close to midnight.

"This won't take too long," she heard him say calmly. "And then I'll walk you home."

The smell of pizza wafted through the apartment reminding Margaret she had eaten very little at dinner. He left the room to return with the pizza and set it on a wooden block in the middle of his tablecloth. "Tuck in," he said, serving her an enormous piece before helping himself to one.

When Matt insisted on walking her home after the meal, Margaret didn't protest too much. Being taken care of was unusual, but it felt very, very nice.

"Margaret." He turned to face her. The hand he placed on the gate into the garden prevented her from going in.

"Yes?" Her heartbeat sounded unusually loud to her. Margaret wondered if Matt could hear it.

"About what I said earlier, I'm sorry if I hurt you in any way. Timmy's lucky to have a sister who cares about him so much."

Margaret didn't say anything. Matt's words were more than generous, but she had things to work out for herself.

He let go of the gate and said, "Good night, Margaret."

"'Night," she echoed, wondering at the strange emptiness she felt as Matthew Magnum walked away.

Chapter Six

"What happened here?"

Margaret looked around Jack and Gina's living room the next afternoon. There was an assortment of packages of all sizes and shapes on the couch and on the carpet. Before Matt could answer her, the doorbell rang. Margaret turned to answer it.

A burly man stood on the porch with a huge rocking chair beside him. Behind him, blocking the end of the drive, was a huge truck.

"Yes?" said Margaret.

"This will come in useful for Jack and Gina's baby, ma'am," the trucker said awkwardly.

He patted the chair while Margaret stared at him. She was beginning to have an inkling where all the presents had come from.

"Who shall I say it is from?" she asked in a daze.

"There's no need to give any name." The man twisted his cap in his hands. "A few of us heard how the baby came early. With Jack and Gina just starting out, we thought they might not have too much money to spare. When Jack told us on the CB that it was a girl...well, I carry furniture for a company in Oregon, and they let me have this chair dirt cheap. Every baby should be rocked."

Margaret's throat tightened as she listened to the trucker's disjointed sentences. The outpouring of caring was hard to believe. "Thank you," she said softly.

Shutting the door, Margaret turned to Magnum. "Are all these gifts from truckers?"

He nodded. "A few are from people here."

Placing the rocking chair by the fireplace, Margaret walked into the baby's room and stopped. Against one wall was a changing table, next to it a chest of drawers. The naked bulb had been removed. In its place, a teddy bear lamp with a cream shade sat on the chest of drawers.

"I don't believe it," Margaret said softly.

"The furniture was dropped off at ten this morning," Magnum said behind her. "The man said his family was complete, and his wife wanted Jack and Gina to have the set."

Margaret shook her head. She had made up her mind to haunt the garage sales in Garrison for furniture and dig through the things in the storage shed in the backyard of The Inner Man, but this exceeded her hopes.

Matt had been busy. The wallpaper border, fixed four feet from the floor, gave the walls the right finishing touch. There was very little, except the trim, left to do.

Picking up a paintbrush, Margaret opened the small can of cream paint. The task would be finished in a couple of hours. There was no need to return tonight. Margaret swallowed hard as the memory of her late-night picnic with Matt returned. Having had a taste of fun, she wanted more.

After finishing the window trim, Margaret decided to take a break before tackling the door. Going into the kitchen for a drink of water, she became aware of a sound on the back veranda. Stepping to the screen door, she stopped abruptly. Matt had his shirt off and was kneeling beside a crib.

Matt heard her come out and stand behind him.

"It's part of the set," he said over his shoulder. "But it needed refinishing."

It had taken him most of the morning to sand the old varnish off. When finished, the crib would look better than new. "What do you think?"

Margaret didn't say anything, and, after a minute, he turned to look at her. Getting to his feet in one lithe movement he asked, "What's the matter?"

As tears streamed down her face, Margaret simply shook her head. Matt wiped his hands on the seat of his pants and cupped her face. "Margaret, what's wrong?"

"I...I'm so happy for Gina and Jack and the baby," she said with a sniff.

Matt smiled. "Let me get this straight. You cry when you're angry, and you also cry when you're happy. Do you ever cry because you're sad, Margaret?"

Margaret gave him a watery smile. "I wanted so badly for them to have nice things for the baby."

"And now they have enough for two babies, maybe even three," Matt said whimsically.

"I'd forgotten how generous truckers are," Margaret said. "When... when my parents died there were so many truckers who didn't know my parents at the funeral. They said they had heard of the accident and wanted to offer their condolences in person. Some of them collected money and gave it to Aunt Jan for us. When they knew she had started a restaurant, they advertised it by word of mouth. For months, she had people stop in and say they had heard about the place from another trucker."

Matt turned to look at her, and Margaret saw the surprise in his eyes. "So, we're not at all bad?"

A part of Margaret echoed Matt's amazement, but she had to set the record straight. "I've never had anything against truckers. How could I? It's only their work that I don't like."

He turned away and she thought she heard a small sigh escape him before he said, "And here I thought you were putting your fears behind you."

"Matt," she said quickly, anxious to change the topic. "About last night. I'm sorry about what I said. I know you don't want to bowl me over, or anything like that."

Their gazes meshed and Margaret felt excitement replace the relief of her apology.

"Margaret, you've got your wires crossed again." Laughter warmed his eyes as he placed his hands on her shoulders. "A part of me does want to bowl you over, but it's not something I can plan cold-bloodedly. It has to happen spontaneously."

"Oh." Margaret's heart raced.

"Have you ever let anything happen spontaneously, Margaret?"

"Like what?" she asked, unable to unlock her gaze from Matt's.

"Like this." His mouth brushed over hers. He lifted his head and looked at her. Margaret closed her eyes and moved closer. Matt's lips closed over hers.

Margaret clung to him as her legs threatened to give way beneath her. Matt's warm mouth felt wonderful; his firm body encompassing hers ignited an ache all over. Margaret slid her arms around his neck, moved her fingers through his hair. Matt hauled her closer.

The doorbell rang.

Matt lifted his head and smiled at her. "Another fairy godmother?" he asked with a rueful smile. "I thought they had to pass a course in timing their appearances before they were given their wands. This one must be a drop-out."

Margaret opened her eyes and looked at him, reluctant to move out of his arms. The thought of a pair of wings and a wand being added to the last burly trucker she had seen made her smile.

"Where did you learn so much about fairy godmothers?" she asked.

"Susan's three-year-old daughter, Melissa Ann," Matt said. "I have to read *Cinderella* to her every night when I visit."

Matt let her go reluctantly and went into the house. Margaret lifted a hand to her mouth. Her lips still pulsed with the warmth of Matt's kiss. With a small sigh, she went inside and returned to work.

Dipping the brush in cream paint, Margaret moved to the door, staring at it dreamily. Heat coursed through her veins, and her palms tingled with the memory of the way Matt's bare skin had felt under them. She closed her eyes.

She was sure Matt would come back to her, that they would continue where they had left off. She waited until she heard the front door shut and Matt's footsteps come down the hall. It took her a minute to realize he had gone past the door.

What did you expect?

Margaret swallowed. Matt's action had cooled her quicker than a pitcher of iced water dumped on her head would.

You enjoyed the kiss but you can't let anything more develop out of it.

Margaret started moving her brush over the door in even strokes. She didn't want her feelings for Matt to develop into anything more serious. In the long, empty months after her parents' death Margaret had realized something. Loving someone exposed one to pain, worry, and the fear of losing them. With the exception of Aunt Jan and Timmy, she didn't want to allow herself to care for anyone else.

* * *

"Hi, Timmy!"

Timmy looked at her and then away as he entered the kitchen and said, "Hi, sis!"

"Going out?" Margaret bit her lip the minute the question was out. She sounded nosey.

Timmy nodded. "T.J. and I are going bowling and then we plan to grab a pizza. I'll see you around, sis."

"Sure," Margaret said.

Her smile faded as soon as the door closed behind her brother. Things weren't getting better. They were getting worse. She had never had any trouble visualizing Timmy as grown up, but she had never thought of growing up as synonymous with losing him.

Her hands trembled as she heated up the clam chowder Aunt Jan had prepared that afternoon. The next few weeks weren't going to be the happy family summer she had envisioned.

Margaret walked over to Joe's after dinner, telling herself all she wanted to do was drop off the linen Aunt Jan had bought for the baby and check if the window and door trim needed another coat of paint. T.J.'s mother had dropped by to visit with Aunt Jan, and the two friends were enjoying their usual gossip over coffee and apple pie.

As Margaret unlocked the front door, Matt stuck his head out of the kitchen. "You're still here?" Margaret asked in surprise.

He nodded. "I wanted to finish the crib today. I've a busy day at the truck stop tomorrow. Come and see how you like it."

Yesterday he had wanted to explain to her that the kiss meant something to him, that it wasn't simply an experiment, but fear had stopped him. His response to Margaret Browning was stronger than he had experienced with any other woman. He couldn't understand why. He only knew he had to take it slow.

Margaret looked at the crib. The newly varnished surface seemed to reflect the rays of the setting sun. "It's beautiful," Margaret said softly.

Matt began to pick up the empty containers of stain and varnish. "Are you in a rush to return, or can you stay? I've got soda in the refrigerator, and we could sit out here for a while."

The heat of the day had given way to a perfect evening. Far away, crickets conducted a symphony. A breeze lifted the loose curls at Margaret's neck and she nodded. "Just for a little while."

Margaret wet her lips as Matt went inside.

Remember he's a trucker at heart. You don't want to feel like this about him.

Feel like what?

Confused, restless, eager.

There's nothing wrong with simply enjoying the man's company, is there?

Matt returned with the sodas to sit down close to her on the back step, without actually touching her. She smelled of summer roses, the kind he had in his garden. She had changed from shorts and a top into a dress. The square neckline emphasized her long, graceful neck. Her hair was tied back in its usual ponytail and the urge to crush his mouth against the loose tendrils at her neck was a powerful one. The cold can of soda in Matt's hand was at odds with the heat inside him. Beside him, he heard the little sigh Margaret gave.

"Tired?" Matt asked.

"Not really. Just content. I'd forgotten how nice summer evenings could be in Inchwater. Washington gets so humid."

"Are you happy you came home, Margaret?"

She nodded. "Yes. Aunt Jan would never have told me how things were with her if I hadn't come home to see for myself. Now I can make sure she doesn't do too much.

She's looking so much better since you found those two women to help her. How did you manage that?''

"It wasn't hard to get word out that Janet is a good employer. Does she always give away more than she sells?''

Margaret nodded. "Yes. You know that old saying; It's not giving that empties the purse? Well, I don't know who coined it, but Aunt Jan definitely proved it right. She has more friends than I know of.''

"You've taken after her, haven't you, Margaret?'' Matt said.

Margaret decided it was time to change the subject. "Aunt Jan told me to thank you the next time I saw you for the roses you sent her this morning.''

"It was my pleasure. Janet was very kind to me when I first came to Inchwater. She encouraged me to make up my mind about having a truck stop here. I think you were very lucky to have her around while you were growing up.''

Margaret nodded. "We were. I remember once when someone at school made fun of us for being orphans. I came home in tears. Aunt Jan told us we may not have parents which, technically speaking, did make us orphans, but we had her, and she was two parents rolled into one. She could spank as hard as any daddy, love as much as any mom. She told Timmy and me, we were lucky. Most kids had to listen to two grown-ups, but we only had to listen to her. She never let us feel sorry for ourselves.''

Lifting her can, Margaret took a sip of her soda. Turning toward Matt, she was struck by his absolute stillness. "Matt, how was your childhood?''

"Terrible.'' He stared into the distance, his expression bleak. "I don't think you want to hear about it.''

Something about the way he looked made her say softly, "Tell me.''

The sound of the can being crushed in Matt's hand made her jump. "Anger ruled my childhood, Margaret. My earliest memory is of my mother and father shouting at each other. They both smelled of liquor all the time, and they were always angry. She used to throw things when she was mad. When she left, I was actually relieved for a while because the house was quiet without her. Susan, Patricia, and I were cared for by an army of servants, and as long as we stayed out of my father's way, we could have anything we wanted.''

The sun sank lower, bathing the back porch in the orange-gold light of predusk. Margaret didn't remove her gaze from Matt's face.

"Each time my father got married, he told us we would be a happy family, that he was doing this to give us a mother. The pattern was repeated twice before I learned nothing was going to change. None of the women cared about us kids. As I grew older, I realized not one of them cared for my father, either, only for what he could give them." Matt's laugh held no humor. "I grew up thinking love was a word a woman tossed at a man to get her own way.''

"That's terrible," Margaret said quietly.

"I've made love to many women, but I've never *loved* anyone. To me, loving someone means handing over control of your life to them and I don't think I can ever trust anyone enough to do that. So, you see, I have my own personal cage, Margaret. One that has made it impossible for me to trust any woman emotionally.''

Margaret swallowed the lump in her throat, not sure what to say. Inane words couldn't heal Matt's mental wounds. She hadn't been through what he had...she could only guess at the extent of his pain. Reaching for Matt's hand where it rested on his knee, Margaret covered it with her own. After a while, he turned his hand upwards and linked his fingers through hers. They sat there in silence while darkness ushered in the stars.

Margaret sat across the kitchen table from Jan. On top of the stove bubbled a huge pot of stew. It had taken the last hour to prepare the vegetables and meat for it, and the aroma was just beginning to seep into the kitchen. Annie, the kitchen helper, had stepped out for her break, and Margaret poured coffee into two mugs. "I'm going over to Gina's after lunch. Do you want me to take anything over?"

Aunt Jan nodded. "I'll give you some stew for Gina, and some for Joe. I'm glad her parents and Jack's go over to visit these days."

"Gina's worried about Jack. She says he's very quiet around her."

Aunt Jan's brow wrinkled in thought. "I wonder what's wrong. They were so happy before the baby got here."

"Jack's taking Gina out to dinner tonight, and she plans on talking to him then," Margaret said. "I'm going to set her hair for her this afternoon."

"Margaret, are you enjoying your vacation?"

"Very much," Margaret said firmly. She could sense the anxiety behind Aunt Jan's question.

There was always something to do. In the mornings, Margaret helped Aunt Jan in the kitchen. Since Gina and Mikki had come home, Margaret spent part of every afternoon with them. In the evenings she read or worked on a new dress she was making. The change of pace from the demands of her job was just what she needed. If only things were better between Timmy and her, Margaret's happiness would be complete.

Aunt Jan sighed. "I'm glad. There's nothing worse than boredom."

"Remember what you told Timmy and me when we were younger?" Margaret reminded her aunt. "Only boring people complain of boredom."

Aunt Jan smiled as she got to her feet, pleased by her niece's words. "I'm glad you decided to come home, Margaret," she said.

Janet had let Margaret think things at the restaurant were getting her down, knowing concern would bring her niece home. Once she had gotten to know Matthew Magnum, Janet had decided nothing else would do but Margaret and Matt should meet. She had done her bit, bringing them together. The rest, she felt, was up to them.

Margaret's thoughts turned to Matt as she set the kitchen table for the evening meal. The last time she had seen him had been at the grocery store, the day after he had finished the crib. He had mentioned he would be away in Los Angeles for a while, and she had nodded casually. A week had gone by, and there was still no sign of him.

Margaret told herself Matt's departure had come at the right time. The last few days she had thought things out and decided he was dangerous to the self-control she had cultivated so carefully over the years. The sensations Matt aroused in her were a result of her lack of experience with men. Just because Matthew Magnum qualified for Kissing Champion of the World was no reason to view him through rose-colored glasses suddenly. Every day, since he had left, Margaret added a new line of her defence of why she should have nothing more to do with Matt.

Matt's involvement with trucking was enough reason for her not to have anything more to do with him. Remembering truckers were nice people didn't alter the fact that the work they did was stressful and dangerous. She could never allow herself to fall in love with a trucker.

Margaret raised a hand to her mouth. What was she thinking of? She did not want to fall in love with anyone, period. Love left one wide open to pain. Margaret lined up her reasons carefully. She had to strengthen her defenses before Matt's return, remind herself of the lessons the past had taught her.

"It's Aunt Jan's night with her International Food Club, isn't it?" Timmy asked, coming into the kitchen. Shower fresh, hair neatly slicked back, he looked very grown-up. "Do we have to eat green noodles and sushi tonight?"

"No." Margaret smiled at her brother. The members of Aunt Jan's club experimented with dishes from different countries each month. "This is Italian month. We've got lasagna for dinner."

"Oh, good!" Timmy handed her his plate, and she placed a generous helping on it, as he helped himself to the salad. "Going out, sis?"

Margaret was surprised. "How do you know?"

"Well, you're usually in shorts and a top, but tonight you're wearing a skirt. Your hair is down, not tied up, and you've got lipstick on."

Timmy bent his head over his food while Margaret stared at him in amazement. There was a time he wouldn't have noticed if she'd worn a toga to the dining table. Timmy's powers of observation had certainly improved.

"I'm going to baby-sit Mikki tonight," she said.

Gina had only agreed to go out with Jack because Margaret had offered to watch the baby. With a typical new mother's fears, she didn't want to trust Mikki to just anybody.

"How are things going at the truck stop?" Margaret asked Timmy casually, serving herself a square of lasagna. The cottage cheese, ground turkey, and Aunt Jan's special sauce made the dish a nutritious and tasty favorite in the restaurant.

"Great," Timmy said. "I went on my first run today with one of the guys. It was just to Barstow and back, but it was neat. The new rigs are something else."

There was a small clatter as Margaret set her fork down. Timmy didn't seem to hear it.

"Mr. Magnum came back this morning from Los Angeles," he said, vigorously shaking pepper over his lasagna. Looking up to discover the reason for her silence he said, "What's wrong?"

Margaret didn't say a word and Timmy's expression changed. "Let me guess. The news that I went on my first run today is too much for you to handle." Angrily he pushed his chair back and stood up. "You're not a good actress, sis. I'll admit you did a fair imitation of accepting it all, but deep inside nothing's changed, has it? You still hate the fact I'm involved with trucking. You want me to stay away from trucks because *you've* never gotten over what happened to Mom and Dad."

"Trucking is dangerous," Margaret said, her head filled with memories of the night Aunt Jan had received the call from the hospital telling her their parents had been in a serious accident.

He stared at her and Margaret realized how stubborn the set of his mouth was. Timmy ran his hand through his hair and turned away to stare out of the kitchen window. "It is not more dangerous than another profession, and I'm sick of you telling me what to do with my life."

Margaret stared at him. Timmy had never used that tone with her before."

"Timmy, we've got to talk."

"What's there to talk about?" he asked. "I'm not going to listen while you try to change my mind. You're scared that I might end up a truck driver like Dad. I'm sorry I can't make things easy by being the nice, safe works-in-an-office engineer you want me to be. I'm not even sure I want to be a truck driver. All I know right now is that I enjoy being around trucks. When the time comes I'm going to choose my own career, whatever it is, not you."

He was gone before all he'd said had fully registered with Margaret. As pain flowed in to replace numbness, Margaret balled her napkin in one hand. Timmy was right. At his mention of going on a run today all her old fears had returned in full spate. She stood up and reached for plastic wrap to cover Timmy's plate. Her own meal she scraped into the trash.

The table cleared, Margaret leaned against the kitchen counter and stared blankly around. It was the first time she had seen Timmy so angry. She couldn't change the way she felt about trucking and if she didn't accept Timmy's love of the work he did she was going to lose her brother completely.

Margaret swallowed the lump of hurt lodged in her throat. Timmy was entitled to make his own decisions. Getting herself to stop worrying was a hurdle she had to overcome by herself.

It was a while before Margaret glanced at the clock. She had promised Gina to be there early.

If only, thought Margaret, as she walked over to Joe's house, Matthew Magnum hadn't chosen Inchwater for his truck stop.

"Hi, Margaret! You're looking very pretty tonight. Want to marry me and live happily ever after?" Joe stood on his front porch. His proposal was in the same tone he had asked her to sell his quota of candy in fifth grade, to raise money for the school band.

"No thanks, Joe. I'm not in the marrying mood tonight," Margaret said with a smile, whisking past him and into the house. "I'm here to baby-sit for your tenants."

"How can a man settle down when his girl won't stay around long enough to accept his proposal?"

Joe's teasing voice followed Margaret to the door of Gina and Jack's apartment.

Chapter Seven

"Hi, Margaret," Jack said, answering her knock on the door. "Come on in."

"Is oo going to say hello to Margaret?" Gina cooed to her daughter, who put two fingers into her mouth and began to suck on them.

"Hello, Margaret!" Matt greeted her, unfolding his length from a chair in the corner to tower over her. "How have you been?"

The foot soldiers, the big guns and the reserve guard of Margaret's defences melted under the heat of Matt's gaze. The color drained from her face. For a moment she forgot all about Timmy and her recent wish that Matthew Magnum had never heard of Inchwater. Emotion pulsed in her throat. She hadn't ever felt as vibrantly alive as she did at this moment. The black-and-white checked shirt Matt wore with black jeans molded his frame, and she wanted to hurl herself into his arms and be held.

Margaret swallowed hard as a picture of Timmy's angry face flashed into her mind. The reminder turned the heat pooling in her stomach to ice.

"Hello, Matt." Her voice held one part reserve, two parts shake.

"Mikki's fed and bathed, so she should fall asleep without a fuss. I've put her in her crib."

Margaret forced herself to look at Gina and concentrate on what she said. "We'll be back by eleven at the latest. If she's hungry..."

"I'll feed her," promised Margaret. "If she's wet, I'll change her, and if she cries, I'll hold her."

Gina nodded and turned to her husband. "Jack, have you left the telephone number of the restaurant—"

"Yes," her husband cut in. "I have, and of the paramedics, the police, your mother, and my mother. I would have left Joe's mother's number as well, only she lives in Arizona." He winked at Matt and Margaret before turning to Gina. "Mikki's going to be fine. Now, let's leave them to it, Babe. Bye everybody and thanks."

Them? Margaret looked questioningly at Matt as Jack whisked his wife out of the room.

Matt raised a brow and smiled. "Gina almost changed her mind about going out tonight, until I told her I would be on hand to help you with Mikki."

The baby's cry cut off the objections Margaret wanted to voice and she turned toward the bedroom. Matt's hand on her shoulder stopped her, and she looked at him.

"What's wrong?" he asked quietly.

"What do you mean?" Margaret made no attempt to keep the stiffness from her voice.

"When you came in, you gave me a glad-to-see-you look. Then suddenly it was as if someone reached out and turned a light switch off inside you, and you could barely stand to look at me. What have I done now?"

Margaret looked at the second button of his shirt. "Timmy went on his first run this morning."

"Ah, I see." Matt's nostrils flared as he removed his hand and stepped back. "You're giving in to all your old fears that something will happen to him just as it did to your parents. You want a fall guy and I'm the one you've decided to pin the blame on for what Timmy is doing."

She stood there, transfixed by the intensity of Matt's gaze. He had guessed right. Mikki's wail, louder and more indignant, brought Margaret back to the present. Hurrying into the bedroom on unsteady legs she picked Mikki up. Margaret cuddled the baby, waiting for her pulse to return to normal.

"Aren't you sleepy yet, huh?" Margaret asked a silent Mikki. The baby stared at her, content now that she had established who was boss.

In the living room, Matt shoved his hands into the pockets of his jeans and admitted the truth to himself. He hadn't been away on business this last week. He'd left to give himself time to get a handle on a strange situation. He couldn't understand the way he felt around Margaret...the longing to hold her, the need to be held by her. His urge to make her aware that she had a life of her own to live had more to it than simply the desire to help another human being.

His interest in her was getting a shade too personal. He had thought being away from Inchwater would give him time to regain complete control of himself. It had worked until Margaret had walked through the door and smiled at him as if he were the best thing that had happened to her all week. It had taken their little argument to cool the heat surging in him.

Returning to the living room, Margaret sat in the rocker and patted Mikki's back. If they were to spend the rest of the evening together, it seemed important to establish some kind of normal tone to their conversation.

Sensing Matt's gaze on her, Margaret said quickly, "Mikki's a very good baby unless she has a touch of colic. Jack and Gina are really lucky. She just wakes up once at night."

"They seem very attached to the baby."

"They are. They argue over who should bathe her or whose turn it is to pick out what she's to wear."

"How many parents really enjoy their children nowadays?"

Mikki gave a huge burp and Margaret said, "That's what was bothering you, wasn't it, sweetheart?" Matt's remark had surprised Margaret. "Most of the parents I know do. What's not to like in a baby?"

"I don't know," Matt said. "But where I come from, I've seen couples separate soon after a baby is born, or they're fighting over whose turn it is to change the baby's diaper, or hold it."

It seemed hard to imagine. "Stress can have that effect on people," she said. Life in L.A., according to what she'd heard, was very busy, very high pressure.

"Wasn't it a strain on Janet raising you and Tim? Yet she talks of both of you with so much love."

Margaret nodded. "I asked Aunt Jan once if it was very hard on her raising us, and she said Timmy and I gave her life focus. The only time she wanted to give us up for adoption was the time we wrote a letter to our doctor, asking him if he would marry her and come be our daddy."

Their laughter mingled in the quiet room, and the baby stirred in her sleep. Margaret patted Mikki's back as she said, "You should have seen Aunt Jan's face when she received a letter from Dr. Bernard, enclosing ours to him. She asked us why we had done it. Timmy said married people had babies, and he wanted Aunt Jan to get married and have a baby, so he wouldn't be the youngest any more and have to listen to everybody. Then Aunt Jan asked for my reason, and I said...." Margaret's voice trailed away as she recalled what she had said. Standing up, she patted Mikki's back and began to walk to and fro with the silent baby.

"What was your reason, Margaret?" Matt asked quietly.

She sighed, aware she had gotten herself into deep waters again. She should have known better than to think Matt would let the matter drop.

Margaret turned away from him and said, "I told her I needed a daddy to give me away when I got married."

There was a silence and then Matt said, "It must have been very hard on you, losing your parents so early."

Margaret swallowed. When her parents had died, she had dealt with the pain by bottling it. Over the years she had refused to uncork the container, fearing the pain once let out would rule her like some malevolent genie. Somehow tonight she could no longer keep the lid on the memories.

"It was." Margaret's voice was barely above a whisper.

Leaving the room, she laid Mikki in her crib and stood by it. The pain she had feared to let out threatened to drown her as Margaret recalled Aunt Jan's face as she had turned from the telephone on that fateful day thirteen years ago.

"There's been an accident," Aunt Jan said, putting her arms around Margaret and Timmy, her lips white.

A light sweat broke out on Margaret's forehead.

One minute she had been a little girl drawing a picture for her mother and father, the next she had turned into some kind of statue, determined not to feel. All she could remember doing was placing her arms around Timmy and saying over and over again. "*I'll* never leave you, Timmy. *I'll* never leave you."

"Margaret."

A warm hand was placed on her back. She didn't want Matt to see her like this. Margaret kept her face turned away, conscious it was wet with tears. She felt Matt's hands on her shoulders, turning her face to face him. His voice, soft and steady, reached out to her. "It's okay to cry."

The simple words, on top of the tension of her argument with Timmy, were her undoing. No one had said them to the stoic little girl Margaret had been. They had all told her to be brave, to take care of Timmy, to be a good girl and help Aunt Jan. No one before Matt had told her it was okay to cry.

The dam of self-control burst, and the pent-up grief of all the years rushed out in full spate. Matt held her close as sobs tore through Margaret. Incoherent words mingled with her tears describing the awful day, the pain, the shock.

Matt's stomach clenched as he listened to Margaret. As she cried in his arms, he wondered if he had done the right thing by forcing her to this point.

When the sobs stopped and she moved away from him, Matt grabbed a couple of tissues from a box on top of Mikki's chest of drawers. Handing them to her, he looked at the sleeping baby. Mikki hadn't stirred through the storm of Margaret's weeping.

"Sometimes, Gina says, Mikki wakes up if anyone sneezes in the other room. At others, a band could play in her room, and she wouldn't hear a thing." Margaret's voice sounded husky, but the quiet humor behind her words filled Matt with gladness.

"Let's go into the living room," he suggested.

He could sense Margaret's embarrassment as she turned from him. He had passed through all the outer layers Margaret had piled on to get to where he was now . . . the threshold of her innermost feelings. One wrong word and she would slam the door in his face.

Matt watched her sit in the rocking chair, her face sad, her eyes filled with memories. He wanted to hold her, but knew it would be better not to touch her just yet.

"You and Timmy were lucky to have Janet," he said. "Nothing can take away the pain of losing your parents, but you have other good memories of your childhood, of growing up with an adult who loved you."

Margaret nodded.

"My best memory is the day I ran away from home." Matt hoped talking would give Margaret the time she needed to calm down. "Susan and Patricia were in boarding school, courtesy of my father's third wife. I had never been lonelier, yet a part of me was glad they had gotten away from it all. There was a big party at our house one night, and my father introduced me to his latest girlfriend who was campaigning to be wife number four and said, 'Meet my son, Matthew. He's a chip off the old block.'

"I stood there shocked by the words. I was nothing like him, but he couldn't see that. I'd told him time and again I wasn't interested in the family business, but he couldn't see that, either. He was very sure that in time I would do exactly as he wanted. Suddenly, I knew if I stayed there any longer I *wouldn't* be able to stop myself becoming like him. The thought of being like my father scared me more than anything else in the world. I went to my room, threw a few things together and slipped out. I hitchhiked to the freeway, more lonely and scared than I had ever been in my life. A truck pulled up after about an hour, and the driver looked down and said, 'Where are you headed, kid?'

"'Wherever you are,' I said, though my teeth were chattering with fright.

"'Want to tell me about it?' he asked.

"'I don't know if it was the darkness or the fact I had never talked to anyone about how I felt, but once I started, I couldn't stop. I let it all out: My father's life-style, how I felt about the women he brought home and our huge house filled with servants and money and emptiness. He listened without saying a word, and when I stopped talking, he pulled up at a truck stop and said, 'We eat and sleep here. First thing tomorrow, you and me are going to talk.'

"The next morning, he told me I couldn't run away from memories, because they were inside my head. The only thing to do, he said, was to face them and realize what could be changed and what couldn't. My father couldn't be changed, which meant I had to change. Then he said, 'Do you know what's waiting for a runaway in the world? More misery and hardship than you've ever thought possible.'

"He gave it to me straight. 'No honest employer will hire you because you're underage. The ones who'll give you work will underpay and overwork you. You'll have to keep hiding and running if you don't want your father to find you. Is that how you want to spend the next few years of your life? And what about your sisters? They might decide to run away, too.'

"I sat thinking about what he had said and didn't like it. But it got worse.

"'You know what?' he said after a while. 'You sound like a rich, spoiled kid to me. In fact, you sound like your father. You say he never thinks of anything but what he wants. Well, you're doing exactly the same thing by running away. Thinking only of yourself.'"

"The shock of being compared to my father frightened me enough to ask the trucker what I should do.

"He said, 'Education and money are your passport to the freedom you want. Go home, finish school, equip yourself with the ability to earn a living. The day you start working is the day you'll begin to have the power to change your dreams into reality. It takes courage and determination to choose a different pattern to the one you've known and stick to it, but it can be done.'

"When he finished talking, he asked me what my decision was. I told him I had decided to go home. He shook hands with me and left me within a mile of my home. I asked him what his name was. 'Bedouin,' he said. 'I've been a rolling stone all my life, and I've never gathered any moss. But you should use what you've got to get you where you want to go. Take the good, ignore the bad. It isn't easy, but neither is the rest of life.' ''

Matt stopped, and Margaret prompted softly, "Go on."

"For years, no one at home knew I had tried to run away. I turned sixteen and got a job that summer working at a truck stop. My father hit the roof when he found out I had no intention of working in Magnum Shipping, but all his hollering couldn't make me change my mind. At eighteen, I left home to go to college and got a part-time job as a mechanic at a truck stop near the university. Later, I was promoted to driver. Bedouin's words proved right. It took college and five years of working as an administration officer in a company to get enough money together for my first truck."

Margaret cleared her throat. "That's why you named your company after him."

"Bedouin did more for me in that one night than my father ever had. He steered me right."

"Did you ever meet him again?"

Matt nodded again. "When I began driving, I asked other truckers about him. One day he called me at the truck stop where I worked, said he'd retired and had a little place by Lake Michigan. I told him what I was doing, how I owed him for what he had done for me. He brushed my thanks away, said I'd always had the potential. I'd just needed to be reminded of it. We talked once a month after that. He died in his sleep a month after I started Bedouin Trucking, but I'm glad he knew that I named my company after him."

A comfortable silence wrapped them while outside the shadows deepened.

"Would you like some coffee?" Margaret asked after a while, and Matt nodded.

As Margaret got two mugs out and waited for the water in the kettle to boil, she thought of what Matt had told her about his early life. Bedouin had had more insight into human life than most psychiatrists.

Matt was standing by the television, glancing through the file she had brought with her, when Margaret carried the coffee in.

"You planned to work tonight?" he asked.

"I just wanted to update the files I've kept since I started working at the Edwards Institute."

"This girl, Vicky Barrows. What's the matter with her?"

Margaret came up beside him and looked at the picture of the blond, smiling twelve-year-old and said, "Vicky has cerebral palsy. She was found abandoned in an old barn a year ago. Dr. Edwards discovered no one had ever tried to communicate with her. At the Institute, she simply lay in bed and stared at the ceiling all day. Dr. Edwards was convinced Vicky could understand what was being said to her, but it had simply become a habit not to respond. I started reading to her, and within a week, Vicky would turn her head and watch the door, waiting for my footsteps each morning. Once she began to react to the sound of my voice and my presence, teaching her became a delight."

"Why is this institute the only one of its kind in the country?" Matt asked.

"Dr. Edwards would like to start another facility, but it isn't easy to find the right person to run it. His job isn't nine to five...it's around the clock, and there aren't many doctors as dedicated as he is."

Margaret didn't mention that she had suggested Inchwater as the ideal place for a second facility because land was so cheap here.

"Maybe I can help."

Hot color stained Margaret's cheeks. "I didn't mean to hint at anything," she said quickly.

"I know you didn't, Margaret, and I'm not offering money. I'm just offering to put Dr. Edwards in touch with someone who could help with the financial expense of a new facility on the west coast."

"Who?" asked Margaret.

"Patricia, my second sister, has made a career out of organizing fund-raisers. She'll be glad to contact Dr. Edwards and talk to him about the kind of work she does."

"If you'll give me your sister's number," Margaret said, "I'll let Dr. Edwards have it and tell him to contact your sister if the idea interests him. He's very firm about the fact that you can't open these centers as if they are fast-food franchises."

Matt hesitated and then nodded. "I'll give you one of Trish's business cards. Her specialty is fund-raising galas with guests paying five thousand dollars a plate for their dinners."

Margaret stared at Matt. The life he talked of seemed beyond her comprehension.

Matt reached up and touched her nose with a finger. "Don't try to figure it out. Trish says she does people in her circle a favor by having these events. By having their donations mentioned by the media, she insists she's building up their self-esteem."

"Dr. Edwards isn't the kind of man to let anyone control him just because they've donated to the cause," Margaret warned.

"The donations are made unconditionally, on Trish's guarantee the funds will be used for the purpose they're intended for."

"It sounds wonderful," Margaret said.

If everything worked out and if Dr. Edwards chose to build a second facility in Inchwater, she could live at home, keep Aunt Jan company.

See Matt every day?

Margaret swallowed. "I'll call Dr. Edwards about what we've discussed."

"How was your trip?" Margaret asked, wanting to change the subject. She regretted it immediately as a vision of Matt in a tuxedo, with a beautiful woman draped on each arm, teased her.

"Very busy. Meetings and work took up so much time I barely managed to get home each night to read my niece her bedtime story."

"You stayed with your sister?" Margaret questioned as the women her imagination had conjured vanished.

Matt shook his head. "Susan, Trish and I have our own places in the nine acres that surround the main house."

Margaret sensed a reluctance in Matt to talk about his life in L.A., and she asked quickly, "Is your niece still insisting on *Cinderella* every night?"

Matt smiled. "She's graduated from *Cinderella* to *Rumpelstiltskin,* which was a bit of a relief."

Margaret considered the different sides she had seen of Matt. The corporate boss, the teasing companion, the good friend. She imagined him patiently reading a fairy tale to a three-year-old. The thought made emotional inroads into her heart. The image of Matt, the man, was taking up more and more room in her thoughts, crowding out that of Matt, the trucking magnate.

They went through her file and Margaret told him a little about each of the ten children she taught.

When they came to the last picture, Matt looked at her. "You love your work, don't you?"

Margaret nodded as Matt went on, "Just like I love trucking."

Margaret's breath caught in her throat. Was there a challenge in the statement? Matt turned to her and said seriously, "I got delivery of a new rig in L.A. Would you like to try it out with me tomorrow, Margaret?"

Margaret swallowed, unable to control the fear that surged in her.

"I'll understand if you feel you can't," Matt said after a moment's silence.

Margaret shook her head. "I'll come with you." Her voice held both fear and resolve.

It was time to stop running.

Chapter Eight

Margaret looked at the heap of clothes on the bed and sighed. Turning sideways, she looked at her reflection in the mirror. The camisole top and jeans she had on wasn't right. None of her other outfits were, either. All fifteen of them.

The tap on her door brought her head around and her breath caught in her throat. Timmy stood in her doorway, looking decidedly uncomfortable.

"Timmy, come in."

He didn't move from his spot by the door. "I just wanted to say I'm sorry for flying off the handle last night."

Margaret swallowed. The olive branch Timmy extended was so frail any attempt to grab it would snap it in two.

"It's all right. I guess from your point of view I do seem paranoid about what you're doing."

She wanted to explain so much, most of all her fear of losing him, but she was afraid to antagonize him again.

"Got to go, sis. Can't be late for work. See you around."

"Bye." There wasn't anything else she could say. Timmy had vanished already.

Margaret turned back to the mirror with a sigh. Even the shade of lipstick she had on looked wrong.

"So this is where you are," Aunt Jan said, coming into the room a few minutes later. "I was wondering about the sounds I've been hearing from here in the past hour. Getting together a collection of clothes for charity, are you?"

"No," Margaret said. "I'm deciding what to wear." She burrowed through the heap on her bed for a scarf.

"What's up?" Interpreting Margaret's look of surprise correctly, Aunt Jan said, "Every time your room looks like the aftermath of an earthquake I know it's because you're in a tizzy about something."

Margaret paused in her search. "Do I really do this regularly?"

Aunt Jan nodded. "It was like this for your first date, then for the prom, then the day you left home for college."

Busy tossing things on the floor, Margaret asked, "Do you think this outfit looks too casual?"

"Depends what the occasion is," Aunt Jan said.

"I'm going for a ride with Matt in one of his trucks."

Margaret missed the way Aunt Jan's eyebrows shot up.

"That's nice." Aunt Jan sounded out of breath. "I have to go now. I think I hear the telephone."

Scarf in hand, Margaret looked up in surprise as the door shut. Which telephone had Aunt Jan heard? The extension at Margaret's bedside was perfectly silent.

Margaret peered into the mirror as she knotted the scarf about her neck. The dark circles under her eyes testified to the anxiety-ridden night she had spent.

"Wouldn't it have been simpler to tell Matt you didn't want to go with him?" Margaret's reflection seemed to ask.

"Well..." Discarding the scarf, Margaret picked up a light cotton jacket and headed for the door. It would have been simpler, but simple wasn't what life was all about.

Margaret watched Matt pull up in front of The Inner Man, her mouth dry. Wiping her damp palms on the sides of her jeans, she thought *I can't do it.* Daddy's truck had been black and white. This one was blue and silver, the shape of the cab entirely different, but the old familiar fears rose up as she looked at it, rooting her to the spot.

I'm going to be sick.

She turned away as Matt jumped down from the cab of his truck and came toward the restaurant.

I have to find Aunt Jan. She'll tell him I'm ill or something.

The yipping stopped Margaret and made her turn slowly around. Matt's arms were filled with a bundle of fur, and two beady eyes stared at her from a mop of a face.

"Where did you find him?" Margaret asked, looking at the puppy.

"He was wandering around the truck stop, completely lost."

Just like she had been that first day. "You think someone abandoned him?"

Matt shrugged. "Could be."

"You could have called the humane society to come and pick him up."

"He seemed so little," Matt said, looking slightly embarrassed. As if on cue the puppy yowled piteously, and Matt patted his head.

"I think he's starving." Margaret reached for a plastic bowl and Ben, the counter boy, quickly handed her a pitcher of milk. Matt set the puppy on the floor and they watched him frantically slurp at the milk, putting a paw into the bowl as if afraid the milk would get away from him.

Margaret smiled. "I think Aunt Jan's got an old basket she doesn't use any more. It would make a nice bed. Let me get it for you."

She returned with the basket and an old cushion to find Matt and the pup out in the yard.

"I didn't want him to make a mess in the restaurant," Matt explained.

They waited while the pup explored the bushes and decided which one he wanted to mark, and then Matt picked him up. "Do you mind if we take him with us?"

"Of course not."

Matt took the basket from her and put it on the floor of the cab. Placing the pup in it, he came around to Margaret's side and opened the door for her. Before Margaret could say a word, he lifted her onto the first step. "Watch your head as you get in," he instructed.

Margaret examined the interior of the cab. Behind their two individual seats in front was another long seat, and beyond that was a curtain.

Matt climbed in, moved to the back seat and said, "Come and look." His voice held all the pride of a child displaying a new toy.

She stood up and slid onto the back seat as he moved the drapes behind it aside. Margaret stared at the made-up double bed that occupied most of the space in the compartment.

"Stereo, refrigerator, television set, even a VCR," Matt said, proudly naming all the accessories in the cab. He pulled out one of two huge drawers under the bed. "Space to keep your clothes. It even has its own door to enter by. Home away from home."

She glanced up at the roof that opened like the moon roof of a car. Imagination immediately supplied a picture

of Matt and herself on the bed, moonlight bathing them
as they made love.

Margaret returned to her seat and sat down abruptly.
Beneath her fingers the rich indigo velour felt soft and very
sensuous. What was wrong with her? It was almost as if
her mind needed washing out with soap. "It's very nice,"
she said blankly.

"When two drivers do the long-distance runs, one usually sleeps while the other drives," Matt said. "Having a
bed in the cab saves time. Even when a driver is alone, he
can pull into a rest area and sleep whenever he's tired
without having to go out of his way to look for a motel."

As Matt started the engine, Margaret glanced out of the
window. There was a perfectly practical explanation for
the bed.

While the engine idled, Matt pointed out instruments on
the seemingly mile-long panel. Steering the truck out of the
parking lot with ease, he glanced at her, but didn't say
anything.

Margaret sat stiffly, hands clenched. The paralyzing
nausea might surface at any minute. As the big rig sped
down main street and merged with freeway traffic, she
continued to wait.

Slowly memories surfaced. Her mother reading to her
as the truck sped down the highway. Herself drawing in the
back seat, or working on the scarf she was knitting for her
doll. Her father pulling up next to a fairground so she
could have a ride on the giant Ferris wheel, then buying her
an enormous candy cane, and showing her how to eat the
sticky confection without getting it in her hair. Timmy
chuckling with delight, his hands on the steering wheel.
Timmy sitting on Daddy's shoulders and saying, "Look,
sis. I'm taller than you now."

Margaret blinked. "I was happy riding with them," she
said on a note of discovery. "*Very* happy."

Matt smiled. It was turning out better than he had hoped. Janet had spoken to him before he'd left the office, made him promise to bring Margaret back if she showed any signs of stress at all. Matt himself had suffered qualms of uneasiness, wondering if he was putting undue pressure on Margaret by inviting her to ride with him. But her words just now assured him everything was going to be all right. Another fragment of the past had surfaced, reminding her that not all her memories connected with trucking were bad.

"The pain of their death formed some sort of mental block in my mind," he heard Margaret say. "How could I have forgotten all the good times we had together? Daddy loved it when we could all accompany him on one of his long trips. I loved it, too."

Over the radio, a husky voice crooned about love and pain. Matt switched it off.

"My mother often rode with him because he was a long-distance driver. It was hard on her leaving us behind, but she told me how lonely it was for Daddy on the road if she wasn't along. She would have only seen him once a month if she hadn't gone with him. I heard her tell Aunt Jan once, the hardest choice she had to make was between her marriage and her children. I didn't understand then, but I do now and I'm glad she made the decision to ride with him."

Silence filled the cab as Margaret finished speaking until Matt leaned forward and flicked a switch. Instantly, a cracked voice came over the air. "This is Lone Wolf. This is Lone Wolf. Ain't anyone listening in? A few more miles without talking to anyone, and my vocal chords are going to atrophy."

Margaret looked at the CB as Matt picked up the handpiece. "Lone Wolf, this is Bedouin Two. Where are you headed for?"

"San Francisco. And yourself?"

"Just up the coast a bit," Matt said. "This is a joyride."

"Oh yeah? Who have you got with you, your sweetheart?"

"Not quite—" Matt exchanged a smile with Margaret, "—but I'm working on it."

Margaret blushed and turned to stare out of the window.

"Well, she could say hello to an old geezer."

Matt held the handpiece out to Margaret, an eyebrow raised in inquiry. She took it from him and said, "Hello, Lone Wolf."

"Hello there, sweetheart. You got a call name?"

Margaret hesitated and then said, "No."

"We've got to have us a christening, then. Can you think of a name, Bedouin Two?" Lone Wolf asked.

"Well," Matt cast a sidelong glance at Margaret as he said, "at times she has a certain keep-your-distance look that reminds me of royalty."

Margaret stared at him. He'd never mentioned her princess look before.

"How about Snow White?" Lone Wolf suggested. Margaret laughed. Matt took the handpiece from her and said, "She's got the most beautiful red hair. Snow White won't do."

Beautiful? thought Margaret. Her carroty curls?

"How about Rose Red, then? Just read my three-year-old grandson that story last night. I keep hiding the book, but he keeps finding it. Damned if I can figure out why the l'il tyke wants to hear that same story every single night."

"Rose Red is fine," Matt said, handing the piece back to Margaret.

"Welcome to the family, Rose Red," said Lone Wolf.

"The family?" Margaret asked.

"That's what we truckers are," Lone Wolf said. "One big family. I won't say happy, mind you, because we're not that all the time, but out on the road when we're alone, the other voices are all we've got. Driving eight to ten hours each day can get pretty lonesome for us long-distance drivers. Some of us don't have anyone waiting for us at home, and our only real connections are our trucking buddies.''

"How long have you been a trucker?'' Margaret asked.

"Forty years. Started when I was twenty and never wanted to do anythin' else. My wife left me for another man because I was never home, but my daughter understands, and I stay with her and her family between trips. This truck means more to me than anything else in the world. Hope I die in it.''

Her father had felt like that about his work, too. She had heard him say once, "A man's got to work at what he enjoys to give it his best.''

"What kind of work do you do, Rose Red?''

Matt listened to Margaret describe her job. Her voice flowed in and around him, wrapping him in its gentleness. He had made it clear to the women he had known in the past that he was not in the running for a long-term relationship. With Margaret, he wanted to build castles in the air. But dreams, Matt knew, could not stay up by themselves. They needed good, solid foundations under them to give them substance. What he didn't know was whether he had what it took to work on those foundations.

"Got to leave you now, Lone Wolf,'' Matt said. "I'm going to get off the interstate here, and head for the ocean on side roads.''

"I know a good place,'' Lone Wolf said. "At 101, instead of crossing the freeway, head south on it for a mile and a half. Park in the rest area there, and go down the slope behind it. When you get to the beach, veer to your right and you'll see a sheltered cove like they have in the movies. Haven't told anyone else about the spot, but a princess deserves a beautiful setting.''

"Thanks, Lone Wolf," Matt said.

"Goodbye, Lone Wolf," Margaret added. "And," she hesitated for a second and then said, "Happy trucking."

"You and Rose Red have a good time, Bedouin Two," Lone Wolf ordered. "Youth doesn't come around twice."

Lone Wolf's directions led them straight to the secluded cove. Aqua waves foamed over each other in their rush to get to shore. The continuously washed sand was very soft and Margaret felt her feet sink in it. In her arms, the puppy wriggled. Nearby gulls tilted their heads inquisitively to gauge the food possibilities of the intruders.

"Set him down," Matt suggested. "He won't get lost here."

The puppy floundered in the sand as he tried to keep up with them. His efforts made Margaret smile. "Have you thought of a name for him?"

"What do you think of Sandy?" Matt asked.

They both laughed as the puppy sat down abruptly, and head tilted to one side, tried to figure out the stuff beneath his feet. Sandy seemed like a perfect name for him.

The cove was hemmed in by huge rocks and the position of the sun made it possible for them to sit in the shade cast by the rocks. Matt spread a cotton rug over the sand and Margaret watched in surprise as he began to unpack a feast from the picnic basket. Aunt Jan's whole wheat rolls and chicken salad, an assortment of deli meats, a thermos of iced tea, homemade cookies and a bag of potato chips.

"Are we ever going back?" Margaret joked.

Matt looked up at her seriously. As their gazes locked, Margaret's heart skipped a beat. The shrill scolding of a gull gave her an excuse to look away. The bird was actually chasing Sandy.

"Shoo!" Running forward Margaret scooped up the whimpering pup. "Did that mean, old bird frighten you,

huh?'' she asked gently. Looking up she found Matt grin-
ning at her.

"What's so funny?" Margaret demanded.

"Do you realize that's exactly the same tone you use
with Mikki?"

"What tone?" she asked bewildered.

"Softy, cuddly, I-think-you're-special tone," Matt said,
pouring milk from a small carton into a plastic dish for
Sandy. "I don't know if our godchild will approve or dis-
approve. Mikela Margaret Wade is under the impression
that only she inspires that kind of affection."

Margaret laughed, sitting down on the rug. She looked
at the dish and then at Matt's face. "Matt, when did you
really get the puppy?"

He noticed her gaze on the milk carton in his hand. For
him to have brought along milk and a dish for the puppy,
finding Sandy couldn't have been a last minute thing.
"Yesterday morning."

"Then why did you bring him along?"

"I thought it might take your mind off the trauma of
riding in a truck again," he said slowly. "I wanted to provide a distraction."

Even before Janet's warning he had thought twice about
what he was doing. Seeing the puppy scampering about his
office, he had brought it along to help distract Margaret.

"Thank you, Matt." Margaret put her hand against his
cheek. Matt turned his head so his warm lips rested against
her soft palm. When he looked at her, Margaret's heart
shied away from the fire that burned in his gaze.

The puppy, meal finished, tried to climb onto Margaret's lap. Margaret patted Sandy's head. Though another
old prejudice had been peeled away, she still hadn't come
to grips with the fear of what Timmy's involvement in
trucking would lead to.

"What's the matter, Margaret?"

She had eaten very little and Matt noticed the way she had become increasingly quiet.

"It's Timmy. He's barely talking to me. I keep telling myself if I don't change my attitude I'm going to lose him, but I still don't want him to have anything to do with trucking."

Matt sighed. "I was hoping today might change your mind."

"It did, but only about one aspect. I discovered I enjoy riding in a truck. Timmy must have memories like I do buried in his subconscious and he's determined to make up his own mind. I can't seem to let go of my fears or bridge the gap between us."

She felt Matt's hand on her shoulder, as he moved his thumb and massaged her collarbone. "Letting go is never easy. A few years back I was exactly in the same spot you are in."

"Tell me about it."

"Susan decided she wanted to join the peace corps when she graduated from college and I was against it, till I realized I was behaving just like my father. It took real effort to remember Susan was entitled to the same personal freedom I had longed for all my life. I told Susan I would support her no matter what. She went off to Africa for two years and was perfectly happy there. All my fears that something terrible would happen to her were unfounded."

"All these years no one has said anything to me about letting go of Timmy." Margaret's voice held one part sadness, two parts anger directed at herself. "Aunt Jan, Timmy, Joe . . . they all felt sorry for me, let me continue the way I was."

"They love you too much to ever do anything to hurt you, Margaret."

She shook her head. "What you did was take a risk, because you're not personally involved."

Matt stared at her. Something told him that he was more involved than he planned to be. He hadn't yet analyzed the way he felt about Margaret... all he knew was she attracted him like no other woman ever had.

"I've been talking to Timmy about college, and he's agreed to take the SAT exams," Matt said quietly. Unless he could recognize what he felt for Margaret without a doubt, he didn't want to discuss it. The mental tug-of-war would take a while to resolve. "I can't promise he'll be an engineer, but I've told him how much my degree helped me in my career."

"Thanks, Matt."

Margaret felt a little better. By the time Timmy got his degree he might change his mind about trucking.

"Timmy's been asking if he can go on one of the overnight trips," Matt said quietly.

Her heart immediately did a tiny flip-flop in protest but Margaret forced herself to say calmly. "I think he'll enjoy that." Learning a new behavior pattern didn't happen instantaneously. It took conscious effort and time.

"I've promised Tim a regular summer job with Bedouin Trucking when he's in college," Matt said. "He might decide trucking is not for him after all, but the fact it's *his* decision will make all the difference to him."

"I know," Margaret said.

After they repacked all the litter and gave the eager gulls the scraps, Matt removed his shoes, stood and held a hand out to Margaret.

"Let's go for a walk," he suggested. Sandy was curled into a ball by the picnic basket, fast asleep. "He'll be fine," Matt said, pulling Margaret to her feet and linking his fingers through hers.

They walked by the edge of the water, the waves washing their feet with an occasional icy offering. After a while, Matt let go of her hand and pulled Margaret into his side.

A light breeze whipped the curls out of Margaret's ponytail and ruffled Matt's thick, dark hair. Above them a gull wheeled and called to its mate. The heat of the sun, the smell of the ocean, the feel of Matt next to her, combined to create a sense of peace within Margaret. It seemed natural to put an arm around Matt's waist, to let her hand cup his side. He felt warm and wonderful.

"Want to go in for a swim?" Matt asked.

"I didn't bring a swimsuit," Margaret replied. "Anyway, I can barely swim enough to keep myself afloat."

They heard Sandy yowling and Margaret said, "Race you back to the cove." She was off and running before she had finished her challenge, but Matt still beat her. Flinging herself down on the rug, Margaret panted, "That's not fair. You have longer legs." Lying on her back, she lifted a hand to shield her eyes from the sun and grumbled, "Aunt Jan's been feeding me too much."

The shadow above her made her lift her hand away, her heart picking up its pace as she saw Matt leaning over her. An arm on either side of her body imprisoned her to the spot.

"Don't be a sore loser, Margaret. It's time to ante up."

She met his smiling gaze and her own shifted to his mouth. It wasn't hard to imagine what he wanted for his prize. Entering into the spirit of the moment Margaret lifted her hands. Placing them on Matt's shoulders she said mock solemnly, "The Brownings of Inchwater always honor their debts."

There was passion in the flare of Matt's nostrils as he looked at her. Lifting one hand from his shoulder, Margaret pressed one finger into the cleft in his chin. His eyes deepened into the color of malachite as he bent his head.

The kiss was an explosion of the feelings that had been building all morning. They lingered over it, pausing only to draw breath and then returning for more. Margaret's hands roamed over Matt's back, urging him forward. Urging him closer.

His mouth left hers to trail kisses over her eyelids, her nose and her forehead. Margaret dragged him back to her mouth with a mew of protest. A little later, Matt's lips blazed a new trail down her neck and then across her chest, following the neckline of her camisole top.

Margaret moaned deep in her throat as sensation after pulsating sensation crashed on the shores of her mind. Drawing Matt close to her, she wrapped her arms around him and held him, her actions clearly conveying she wanted more. "I want you Matt," she whispered.

Suddenly she felt him stiffen, then he was turning away.

"Matt?" She sat up confused, wondering if she had dreamed the last few moments.

"It's getting cold out here. We had better leave." She stared in disbelief as he picked up the hamper and Sandy, and walked off. He couldn't have moved faster if she had been a skunk with her tail lifted.

Margaret got to her feet and folded the blanket. On legs that shook, she walked after him wishing she could burrow into one of the tiny shells in the sand and never have to face Matthew Magnum again.

What on earth had made her come across so strong? *I want you Matt*. Margaret's face burned at the memory. His rejection stung. Just because his kisses made her feel like a femme fatale, didn't mean she was one. How could she have broken a personal rule of never coming on to a man?

Margaret scrambled up the slope, ignoring the hand Matt stretched out to help her and clambered into the truck. In her seat, Margaret leaned back and closed her eyes. Shame wasn't a good medium to fry in.

Matt stared at the road ahead, his brows drawn together. He had wanted one kiss, but her response had made him hurl caution to the wind and take more than he meant to. Under different circumstances, with someone else, he would have made love on the beach without a second thought. Only Margaret was entitled to more than a few moments of stolen pleasure. He threw her a quick glance. Eyes shut, head tilted back against the seat, she looked lost and lonely.

Chapter Nine

"Margaret, I'm sorry."

She kept her eyes closed. The words were a figment of her imagination, the same way she had imagined that he wanted to make love to her.

"Margaret, we have to talk."

She remained stubbornly silent. A second helping of humiliation would be too much to handle.

"Margaret, I want you as much as you want me."

Margaret opened her eyes and looked at Matt as he said, "Have you changed your mind about being personally involved with trucking?"

"I don't know," Margaret said slowly.

She hadn't been thinking back then, simply concentrating on the feelings Matt aroused in her.

"I'm a trucker at heart, Margaret. Lately I've been busy at the truck stop, but when things settle down and I hire more staff, I intend to go back to driving one of my trucks from time to time. It's what I like best. For our relationship to be a success, you will have to accept me as I am . . . seventy-five percent trucker, twenty-five percent a society figure."

Margaret didn't say anything and Matt went on.

"It would be easy to take what we want now and think later, but I can't do it. All through my childhood I saw what happened when my father did just that. You're not the type to come through an affair unscathed, or go into one just for the temporary pleasure it would bring you and I'm not ready to make a permanent commitment, yet. We both have personal conflicts to resolve before we can go on."

She shouldn't resent his clear way of analyzing the situation. The lessons branded on Matt's mind as a child made him the way he was. Unusual, different, *special.*

"I don't want a permanent commitment." The minute the words were out, Margaret swallowed. She had wanted to make it clear she wasn't trying to trap him into marriage, but now it sounded as if all she did want was an affair with no strings attached.

Margaret closed her eyes. Should she tell Matt her deepest fear was that of losing the ones she loved? Avoiding love was her only guarantee against pain. As long as her emotions were carefully locked away, as long as she didn't depend on anyone for her happiness she would be safe.

Margaret wondered how Matt would react if she shared her thoughts with him, but stubbornness kept her quiet. This was one problem she was going to work through herself.

"Have you had any luck with catching the people who are stealing from you?"

Clever, Margaret, really clever.

As a red herring, it wasn't the greatest, but Matt apparently sensed her need to veer away from the personal.

"I have a hunch it's happening at one particular truck stop near Vegas," Matt said, checking his huge side mirror before changing lanes. "My drivers are watching the spot, but so far no one has been caught. Last week a carton of computer disks was missing from our delivery. Our insurance covers the losses, so the companies we deliver to have no complaints, but it still bothers me that it's happening."

Margaret wondered what Matt planned to do after he caught the thieves. Would he return to L.A.? The summer was half over and soon she would have to think of returning to Washington. Confused and tired, Margaret closed her eyes.

Matt leaned forward and flicked on the CB. As they sped along, Margaret listened to voices over the air, discussing last night's basketball game. Suddenly, a new voice cut in. "Breaker. Breaker. There's a trucker in trouble on Brown Road, just off the 101 Freeway, south of San Luis Obispo. He just reported a 1033. Driver's young and scared. Anyone in the area?"

Margaret's gaze flew to Matt as he reached forward and picked up the handpiece. She knew a 1033 was a dire emergency. "This is Bedouin Two. I'm ten minutes away and heading there right now."

He drove in silence, concentrating on the road. Five minutes later, they saw the truck. Matt pulled up behind it and let out a long whistle. The flatbed's load was tilted at a dangerous angle. The driver was lucky the rig hadn't overturned.

"Stay here," Matt told Margaret, getting down.

Margaret checked the puppy and then opened the door on her side. Maybe there was something she could do to help.

Matt approached the driver and held his hand out. "Magnum," he said in brief introduction. "How did this happen?"

As the driver mumbled an explanation Margaret glanced at the woman and child sitting on the roadside. Their dark eyes watched her, identical expressions of worry in them, but they didn't return her smile.

"Are you all right?" Margaret asked softly.

They continued to stare at her and she realized they didn't speak English. Margaret's Spanish was limited. She glanced over her shoulder to where Matt and the driver examined the ropes that bound the load to the flatbed.

Margaret looked back at the pair and noticed the moisture in the woman's eyes. "Don't worry," she said softly.

The woman looked away from her, holding her child closer, and Margaret got to her feet slowly. They both looked cold in their thin, cotton clothing. Going to the truck, she picked up the blanket and hamper and walked back to the mother and child.

Shaking the blanket out, Margaret placed it around their shoulders, then opened the hamper and took out the packet of cookies. The little boy's eyes grew large as she offered them to him, but he looked at his mother for permission before taking one. Margaret poured coffee from the thermos into the cup for the woman, adding a packet of sugar to it. Something hot and sweet would combat shock.

"It's going to be a while," Matt said behind her, and Margaret got to her feet.

"What's wrong?"

"The load's too big, which explains why the driver was using side roads at this hour. He has to avoid the weigh stations that check loads. The winds have picked up, and he says the truck almost went over at the last curve. If it had, he and his family might have been killed, not to mention the danger to any other vehicles and passengers." She had never seen Matt so angry. "It's going to take a while to secure the load again. I hope you don't mind waiting."

"I'm fine," Margaret told him. "Go ahead and do what you have to."

As Matt nodded and turned away Margaret heard a sharp yipping from the truck. The little boy looked in the direction of the sound, his eyes rounded in wonder. Fetching Sandy, Margaret put the puppy beside the boy. He looked at her, and then hesitantly raised a hand to pat the puppy, his solemn face creasing in an enormous smile.

"Sandy," Margaret said pointing to the puppy, and the little boy repeated the word.

"Sandy."

Margaret nodded and the little boy's face lit up. He pointed to himself. "Juan," he said shyly.

"Hi, Juan!" Margaret said.

The pleased giggle the boy gave coaxed a hesitant smile to the mother's face. Margaret sat down beside them, pouring another cup of coffee for the woman, watching Juan play with the puppy.

It took an hour before Matt and the father stopped working and came towards them.

"*Señor*, thank you very much," Margaret heard the man say twice.

"It's all right," Matt said briefly, and Margaret could still hear the lingering anger in his voice.

He stopped beside her and looked at the little boy who held the puppy in his arms, while the man spoke to his wife in Spanish.

"Margaret, this is Ramon," Matt said in introduction, when they'd finished talking.

"We have not been here long in this country," Ramon said. "My wife and son do not know English, but my wife, she says your kindness can be understood in any language, *señora*. We all thank you."

Ramon said something to his son, and the boy's face lengthened as he looked at the sleeping puppy in his arms. They saw his mouth quiver as he gave the puppy one last hug. Margaret met Matt's gaze, and as he raised a brow questioningly, she nodded.

"If your son would like the puppy, and you can take good care of it," Matt said, "I would like him to have it."

Margaret watched the little boy's face light up as his father translated what Matt had said. The child nodded eagerly and the woman smiled as Ramon turned to them. "Thank you *señor*. My son is lonely since we left Mexico. Maybe the puppy will make him happy again. He has much love to give it."

He helped his wife and child into the cab. Margaret stood beside Matt, and they watched the rig pull out into the freeway with a final toot of thanks.

Matt turned to Margaret. "Tired?"

She shook her head. "I'm glad we could help."

Recalling the worry in the wife's face, the fear in the child's, she hoped life would be kind to the immigrants. Glancing at Matt, she noted the tightness around his mouth.

"Why are you angry?" she asked.

"I'm angry with the type of employer Ramon has," Matt replied. "A man who risks lives just to transport a bigger load and get more money should be reported. He's the kind who forces his employees to drive longer hours and falsify the logs they keep. Drivers like Ramon are too new and scared to report him to the proper authorities. I bet Ramon isn't even paid the regular wage."

"What can you do about it?" Margaret asked.

"I got the man's name from Ramon," Matt said. "I'm going to call him and tell him my drivers are going to keep a lookout for his trucks. If he doesn't start complying with safety regulations immediately, I'm going to report him. He's a black mark on the industry."

Margaret stared out of the window at the reflectors gleaming on the surface of the road. She thought of one of the first things Matt had said to her.

I care about you and Timmy the way any decent human being cares about another.

Caring, for Matt, didn't stop with the people he knew. It extended to every human being, no matter what his race or color. It was a rare quality, Margaret realized, in a day and age where people seldom thought of anything but themselves.

Margaret rocked Mikki in her chair while Gina folded the laundry.

"How are things with you and Jack?" Margaret asked. Gina had been unusually quiet today.

"All he talks about is freight and deliveries," Gina said. "I know we need the money, but Jack's working as if the president's made him personally responsible for the national debt."

As Margaret walked back to The Inner Man, she wondered if his job was responsible for Gina and Jack's problems. She recalled Matt's words.

I'm seventy-five percent trucker, twenty-five percent a society figure.

Matt hadn't only pointed out her own fears, he had acknowledged his own, as well. Margaret wondered what it would be like to be married to Matt. Imagination provided her with pictures of Matt coming home to her, playing with their children, loving her. Hot color rose to her cheeks as she thought of that warm mouth against her skin. Matt's sensitivity would make him a great lover, but dreams needed hard work to turn them into reality.

Margaret spent the evening cutting out a pattern for a dress and then she went downstairs to the garden. Timmy was out and Aunt Jan was talking to some of her customers in the restaurant.

She was flipping through a magazine when a movement by the gate caught her eye. Margaret lifted her head just in time to see Timmy retreat hurriedly.

She swallowed. Her brother seemed determined to avoid her. With her foot, Margaret set the swing in slow motion oblivious to the beauty of the perfect summer evening. All she was aware of was the fear wedged in her heart that Timmy and she were growing further apart each day. Her mind challenged her to look at the situation from both sides.

How can I take care of him if he won't let me?

It wasn't a lifelong position, though you thought it would be. Timmy's old enough to take charge of his own life.

What if he fails?

He has to learn to pick himself up, dust himself off and get on with the business of living. It goes with the adult territory.

The creak of the garden gate brought her head up.

"Matt."

"Hello, Margaret."

She wore a pale cream sundress. Narrow straps drew attention to her beautiful shoulders. With the setting sun turning her hair to flame, she looked very tempting. Matt wanted to move the hair from her shoulders aside, place his mouth against the slender column of her neck, and let feeling drown his thoughts out for once.

"Aunt Jan's in the restaurant," Margaret said.

"I came to see you." Matt handed her the single rosebud he had picked from the garden. Its fragile beauty reminded him of Margaret. Soft, delicate, *shy.*

None of the women he'd known had ever been shy. She looked at the rosebud and then at him, color staining her cheeks. "Thank you, Matt. Would you like to sit down?"

Ignoring the two redwood chairs, Matt nodded and sat on the swing next to Margaret.

"So, what have you been doing with yourself today?" he asked lightly.

"Nothing much. I spent the afternoon with Gina and Mikki. Have you noticed anything different about Gina and Jack?"

"No. Why?"

"Gina's worried that Jack may not care for her anymore."

"That's ridiculous," Matt declared. "Why, he's working his tail off to make sure she and the baby have all they need."

"Matt, he barely speaks to her."

"Just because he's not around to fall in with her wishes, Gina is feeling insecure. Women hate to lose control."

"Don't you dare compare Gina to the women you knew," Margaret snapped. "She is not trying to control Jack."

"What is she trying to do, then?"

"She just wants him to work less, spend more time with her and the baby."

The light in Margaret's eyes warned Matt he was in trouble. He tried to change the subject. "The man's probably tired when he comes in and doesn't feel like talking."

"How much energy does it take to say 'I love you'?" Margaret demanded.

Matt looked at her sparkling eyes and angry mouth and asked, "Has anyone said it to you, Margaret?"

"N-no."

Matt wondered what it would be like to say those words to her. He couldn't say them, though, until the words would signify a love that would last them for the rest of their days.

"There you are," Janet said, coming out into the garden. "Why, Matt, how nice to see you. As hard as you work, it's good to know you're taking time to relax as well. Mac tells me though you pay for a room in his motel, you really live at the truck stop."

"Relaxing is only possible in the right surroundings and with the right company." Matt glanced at Margaret.

"True." Janet beamed at him. "I suppose that's why Margaret insists on us making a trip to Yosemite National

Park. It's the only place I sit around and do absolutely nothing.''

"It's hard to imagine you doing nothing," Matt said.

"Would you like to come with us to Yosemite?" Janet asked suddenly. "Timmy's going to stay here, but the cabin Margaret's rented sleeps four easily.''

Matt couldn't make out Margaret's expression. Her head was bowed over the rose she held.

"When are you going?" he asked.

"We're leaving Monday after next, and we'll be there for a couple of weeks.''

"I'm afraid I won't be able to get away then. There are a couple of conventions I have to attend in L.A. during that period.''

"Matt, Joe told me you've bought some land here. Are you planning to expand your truck stop?''

"No," Matt replied, aware of Margaret's surprised gaze on him. "I'm planning on building a house.''

"You sound as if you've decided to stay around Inchwater, Matt," Janet said.

He hesitated. "Inchwater kind of grows on you. Everyone tells me there's nothing much here and yet it seems to have everything I want. A slower pace, a way of life where people have time for each other.''

Janet got to her feet. "Eight o'clock. It's time for my show. Excuse me, won't you?''

She was gone before either of them could say anything. Matt smiled at Margaret. "She's never run off like that before.''

"It's her favorite show and she doesn't like missing any of it.'' Margaret's mind wasn't on Aunt Jan's hasty retreat. It was on Matt's decision to settle in Inchwater.

"Have you heard from Dr. Edwards?''

Margaret shook her head. "He won't rush into a decision.''

"An Institute here would change things in Inchwater. More jobs would bring in more people, maybe even attract a developer or two. Does the thought of Inchwater changing bother you?" Matt asked.

Margaret shook her head. "I don't think we will ever become a big city, but the Institute will provide jobs and pave the way for facilities we've had to do without all this time. It would be nice to have an elementary school and a medical clinic here."

"You won't blame me, then, for Inchwater changing?"

Margaret wasn't sure if she imagined the hint of watchfulness in Matt's eyes.

"Like I blamed you about Timmy working at the truck stop? Aunt Jan told me yesterday how worried she was about the boy Timmy had started hanging out with in Dan's Donuts."

"Have you had a chance to talk to Timmy and tell him what you told me on the beach?" Matt asked. "That after he gets a degree, you won't object to any career he chooses?"

Margaret shook her head. "Not yet. I don't want to risk wording it wrong and upsetting Timmy more."

Matt placed an arm around Margaret's shoulders and it seemed natural to move closer and rest her head against his shoulder. There was comfort in his warmth, in the tenuous peace between them.

Janet Hooper peeped out a little later from an upstairs window and smiled. She'd wondered how long it was going to take those two to realize they were made for each other.

Busy peeling shrimp at the sink, Margaret didn't look up when the telephone rang at eleven the next morning.

"Margaret!" The tone made her spin around. Aunt Jan stood by the kitchen telephone, her face white. She stared blankly at the pie crust she had been rolling, then at the peaches simmering on the top of the stove, as if she weren't quite sure where she was.

"What's wrong, Aunt Jan?" Margaret quickly washed her hands and went to her side. "Are you in pain?"

"It's Timmy," Aunt Jan said blankly.

"What about Timmy?" Margaret asked over the sledgehammer strokes of her heart.

"That was the Las Vegas police. Timmy has been admitted to Las Vegas General Hospital with minor injuries. He is with one of Matt's drivers, Bud someone-or-other." Aunt Jan sank into a chair, removed her glasses and pinched the bridge of her nose. "I can't bear it if anything happens to Timmy."

Margaret knew Aunt Jan loved her as much as she did Timmy, but Timmy had been Aunt Jan's baby.

Automatically, Margaret put an arm around Aunt Jan's shoulders and steered her to a chair. "Don't worry. If it was really serious, the police would have told you. We'll leave for Las Vegas immediately."

Aunt Jan looked at her and said, "I can't go with you. I just can't. I'll wait by the phone."

The words made Margaret realize Aunt Jan feared the worst. The last few minutes had drained her of all her normal vitality. She looked old and helpless, just like the time she had heard of her sister and brother-in-law's death. Margaret's own mind replayed a similar scenario.

"Oh, Timmy." Aunt Jan closed her eyes as if to block out the thoughts.

A fierce tide of protective love rose in Margaret. "Timmy will be fine," she said firmly. "I'll call as soon as I see him."

Aunt Jan nodded vaguely as Margaret looked around for the bag she had dropped on the counter when she returned from the store that morning. Spying it under a newspaper, Margaret picked it up. Bending to kiss Aunt

Jan's cheek, she said, "I'll call you as soon as I get there. Try not to worry too much."

Going into the restaurant, Margaret told Stacey O'Hara, one of the new employees, what had happened.

"Don't you worry about your aunt," Stacey said immediately. "I'll stay with her till we hear something."

"Thanks," Margaret said, heading for the door. Hurrying out to where Beelzebub was parked, she flung her bag onto the back seat and got into the car.

Margaret rested her head against the steering wheel for a minute, willing herself to stop shaking. She saw herself standing by her parents' grave with Aunt Jan and Timmy. Aunt Jan's face as it had been a few minutes ago popped into her mind. Frantic, desolate, *withered*.

Please don't let anything happen to Timmy.

It took exactly four minutes to get to the truck stop. As Margaret got out of the car, Matt came down the steps of the front office toward her.

"Have you heard anything?" she demanded.

"Timmy's injuries aren't serious. I spoke to a doctor in Las Vegas General and the police. It seems Timmy surprised the burglar as he was attempting to remove a box from the trailer."

All Margaret's mind saw was Timmy lying in a bed, in a body cast.

"How could you deliberately let Timmy go on that run when you knew it was dangerous?" she asked bitterly.

Matt put his hands on her shoulders. "Listen to me, Margaret—"

She moved away from him. "No, you listen to me, Matt. You had no business sending Timmy to Vegas."

"Margaret, I didn't even know he was on that run till I got the call from Bud Hancock, the driver of the rig, a while back."

Tears blurred her vision, and she turned away to her car. Recriminations weren't any use now. She had to get to Timmy.

"Margaret, come with me. I am leaving for Vegas immediately."

"You've done enough," she flung at him. "Just stay away from us in the future, Matt. I should never have listened to you in the first place. I knew no good would come of Timmy getting involved with trucking." Angrily, Margaret turned the key in the ignition. Beelzebub refused to start. Trying again and again, Margaret finally got out of the car and slammed the door.

"Margaret, come with me," Matt repeated.

It was better than wasting time persuading someone else to take her in to Las Vegas. On her way here, she had passed Joe, lying under his jacked-up car. Waiting for him to put the wheels back on would take too long. She really had no choice except to go with Matt.

Chapter Ten

Heading for Matt's car in silence, Margaret got in brushing her tears aside. Timmy couldn't die now. She wouldn't let him.

"The bump on Timmy's head is the size of an egg," she heard Matt say quietly. "An X ray has revealed no internal injuries."

What did he know? There were cases where a person with head injuries went into a coma years later for no apparent reason. There were cases . . .

Stop it. You're making a mountain out of a molehill. If Timmy wasn't all right, Matt would say so.

Margaret swallowed. Matt had never lied to her about anything. As some of her fear receded, she recalled something Matt had said earlier. He hadn't known that Timmy was on this run.

Margaret moved restlessly on her seat, stealing a glance at Matt's profile. Why had she blamed him for Timmy's mishap without waiting to check her facts out?

Margaret sighed. It had to do with having red hair. It had to do with not having let go of her brother yet.

Timmy has a lump the size of an egg on his head. Matt's calm, measured tones had told her the exact extent of her brother's injuries. Timmy had been hurt worse when he had fallen out of the apple tree in the backyard and broken his arm. Then there was the time he had fallen off his skateboard and got a bump the size of an ostrich egg on his forehead. She hadn't blamed anyone on those occasions.

You flew off the handle without any cause didn't you?

Closing her eyes, Margaret admitted she had. How could she have hurt Matt so badly?

"Matt," she put her hand out and touched his arm. "I'm sorry I said what I did at the truck stop."

"That's okay, Margaret. You were scared."

His voice frightened her. It was the tone of a stranger. Reserved, formal, *aloof*.

Margaret swallowed hard. "Timmy chose to go on the trip, and no one is responsible for what happened to him. The shock of the news and seeing Aunt Jan so upset made me overreact, but that's no excuse for attacking you. Forgive me."

"Don't worry about it." He sounded weary, as if he didn't want to discuss the subject any more.

Margaret wanted to say something, anything, but the words died in her throat. The stranger who sat beside her wouldn't encourage conversation.

A glance at her watch revealed that it was half an hour since they had left Inchwater. They should be in Las Vegas in two hours. Leaning back in her seat, Margaret closed her eyes.

Why had she lashed out like a wild animal in pain?

I knew no good would come of Timmy being involved with trucking.

Margaret cringed in her seat. That one statement must have convinced Matt she had lost none of her fears about trucking. She ought to tell him it wasn't trucking she was scared of, it was the fear of losing her brother, period. The dread that the same fate that had snatched her parents away was also reaching out for Timmy had made her blind to everything else. Fear had snapped the bonds of self-control and she had lashed out at Matt.

Matt probably thought all she had said about coming to terms with Timmy's choice of occupation was just a front. Margaret bit her lip. He must think she was like the women his father had married who would say anything to get what they wanted.

She was back to square one, and whereas the first time around Matt had been there to help her, now Margaret knew she was absolutely alone.

They stopped at a fast-food restaurant halfway to Las Vegas. Matt bought himself coffee, and Margaret had a glass of lemonade. She stared at him and wished life came equipped with rewind and erase buttons. She would give anything to wipe out the last hour from Matt's memory.

Timmy was the sole occupant of a room with two beds. He was sitting up watching a music video on television when they pushed open the door of his room.

"Timmy, are you all right?"

The sight of the bandage around his head and his paler than normal face worried Margaret. The flood of relief bubbling up in her that his condition wasn't worse brought tears to her eyes.

"Hi, sis! Hi, Mr. Magnum!" Timmy flicked the television set off. "You didn't have to come out here. I'm fine."

"Your sister was worried about you." Margaret heard the reproof in Matt's voice.

Tim seemed to hear it, too, because he said, "I'm sorry, sis. All I meant was, I'm not hurt bad or anything."

Margaret looked at him. "Are you sure?"

Timmy nodded. "I'm sure."

Margaret blinked backed the tears. "I'll call Aunt Jan and be right back. She was worried sick."

"I've already called her," Timmy said quickly. "After my doctor talked to Mr. Magnum, he came in and said Mr. Magnum wanted me to call Aunt Jan and you. She told me you were already on your way here."

Warmth wrapped Margaret's heart. Matt had been thinking of them even then. Feeling worse than before, Margaret sat down on a chair beside the bed.

"What happened?" she asked Timmy.

"Bud and I stopped at this rest area thirty miles outside Vegas. First, I thought I'd get a soda, then I changed my mind and decided to return to the truck. I heard some kind of sound from the rear, and I went toward it. I just caught a glimpse of this man fiddling with the lock before he pushed me over and ran. I hit the back of my head when I fell."

Margaret swallowed hard. What if the man had had a weapon. What if...?

Matt's hand on her shoulder brought her back to the present in time to hear Timmy say, "...and the police got a report from me after the doctor checked me out. Dr. Patterson wouldn't allow the newspaper reporter to talk to me, though."

Timmy didn't sound too happy about being deprived of his shot at fame.

A sound at the door drew their attention to it. A nurse bustled in, placed a thermometer in Timmy's mouth and took his pulse.

Glancing at them she asked, "Your family?"

Timmy nodded and Margaret said, "I'm Tim's sister, Margaret Browning, and this is a friend, Matthew Magnum." She hoped the last part was still true.

"Stop by the nurses' station at the end of your visit, will you?" the nurse said.

"You mean I'm not leaving with them?" Tim asked as the thermometer was removed.

The nurse shook her head firmly. "Dr. Patterson wants to keep you overnight for routine observation."

"Oh, man!" Tim sank against his pillows, the epitome of teenage frustration.

"One night of rest will have you feeling like new," the nurse said. "The sedative I gave you is going to make you very drowsy. Don't fight it. Before you know it, it will be morning and you'll be out of here."

Timmy groaned as the door shut behind her. "I wanted to get back to Inchwater tonight. Jack said he'd take me to Los Angeles tomorrow."

Margaret bit down hard on her lower lip to stop the protest that immediately sprang to her lips.

"No more runs till I say so, Tim," she heard Matt say. "You'll have to rest for a few days to make sure you are absolutely well. I don't want Margaret and Janet worrying about you."

There was no mistaking the authority in Matt's voice. Tim stared at him in surprise and then said very quietly, "Yes, sir."

Matt and Margaret said their goodbyes half an hour later when they saw Tim's eyes begin to close. Bending to brush a kiss on her brother's forehead, Margaret said, "Bye Tim. We'll be back first thing in the morning."

Tim actually raised his hands, placed them around her shoulders, and kissed her on her cheek. "Bye, sis. Bye, Mr. Magnum."

Margaret walked out of the room dazed by her brother's show of affection. It had been so long since Timmy had voluntarily made a gesture of affection.

The nurse looked up as they stopped at her station. "Got a message for you here somewhere. Ah, here it is." She handed over an envelope and said, "It's from the police department. An officer dropped it off fifteen minutes ago. Didn't want to mention it in front of Tim and get him all worked up. He's very excited about what happened, as it is.''

Matt ripped the envelope open as Margaret said, "Is he really all right?"

"Fit as a fiddle," the nurse said. "It's routine to keep head injuries overnight, to make sure there's no concussion or after effects. Come by for him at eleven tomorrow. Dr. Patterson makes his rounds at ten, and he will sign the discharge papers then. The doctor left his number in case you want to talk to him personally. Mr. Magnum told him he was bringing you here, and he would appreciate the doctor making himself available to talk to you. You're a lucky young woman to have a man like that."

Margaret looked at Matt. Yes, she was lucky. He had done everything he could and more to help. She wondered if he would ever forgive her. He looked up at her, and she said quickly, "I think I'll find a . . ." The rest of the words died on her lips as she saw his face. "What is it?"

"They want me to go down to the police station in the morning. They've picked up a man fitting Timmy's description of the suspect, who's confessed to the burglaries."

Margaret stared at Matt in surprise. "That's quick work."

He folded the note and slipped it into the back pocket of his jeans. "It is."

"Where to, next?" Matt asked as they left the hospital parking lot.

Margaret looked away quickly. "If you'll just drop me at the first motel we come to, I'll check in. Tomorrow, I can rent a car before picking Tim up at the hospital."

"I'm not going to leave you here alone. Besides, I have to go to the police station in the morning. We'll both check into a motel, and then I want to show you Vegas. It's not a city one sleeps in at night.''

Margaret took a deep breath. ''You aren't angry with me any more?'' Her cautious tone revealed both question and wonder.

''If danger had threatened Susan or Patricia, and I thought you were responsible, I would have lashed out exactly as you did.''

Margaret swallowed the lump in her throat as the light changed and the car sped forward. Matt understood why she had reacted like she did, and that was important.

''So, will you let me show you Vegas?'' Matt asked.

''I don't have anything to wear for tonight.'' The shorts and top she was wearing were hardly appropriate.

''We'll go shopping for an outfit and pick up some toilet articles, as well, before we find a place to stay. What do you say to staying at a casino on the Strip?''

Margaret nodded. She had never been to Las Vegas before, but she had heard enough about that section of Las Vegas Boulevard called the Strip to know it was the center of all the activity.

Matt pulled up at a shopping plaza, and Margaret picked out an embroidered cotton dress, an oversized T-shirt to sleep in, and a few other necessities, paying for them with her credit card, while Matt made his own purchases.

He picked a casino for them to stay at and, while he asked for two rooms, Margaret looked around, fascinated. Millions of lights, the sound of money falling out of slot machines, the smell of smoke, the sight of the waitresses in their skimpy costumes, people everywhere. The inside of the casino looked like a movie set.

''Come on. We've got rooms at the back where it's quiet.''

Separated from the main casino by the swimming pool, their rooms were on the ground floor of a building at the rear.

Matt opened her door, and then stood aside and handed her the key to her room. "Take a nap if you want to," he said. "I'll be at your door at eight."

Asking room service to call her in an hour, Margaret lay down on the double bed, intending only to stretch out for a few minutes. She reached up and rubbed a hand against her forehead. So much had happened since this morning and her mind, as usual, was doing its juggling act, tossing thoughts at her like colored balls.

Her first reaction to the news that Timmy had been hurt was that she wanted him to be all right. It was the most important thing in the world to Margaret. Nothing else mattered, beside that. Timmy could decide to set up a grocery store on the moon and she wouldn't mind, as long as he was well and happy doing it.

Margaret closed her eyes. She finally knew what she wanted to tell her brother.

The ringing of the telephone woke Margaret at seven-thirty. After a cool shower, she got into her new dress. The bright flowers on the white background made it look smart enough to go out in. The white hoop earrings she had picked up on impulse, added just the right touch. Maybe it was the atmosphere of Las Vegas, but she wanted to look different tonight . . . more sophisticated, more sure of herself.

Brushing her hair, Margaret gathered it into a loose knot at the top of her head, pinning it securely. It left her neck bare and cool. Using the powder compact and lipstick in her bag, she stood back, eyed her reflection and frowned. It looked as if a dozen freckles had appeared since this morning to keep the others company.

The knock on the door came a second later. Heart beating, Margaret hurried to open the door. Matt looked at her and held a hand out. "You look lovely."

Margaret's heart picked up its pace as she put her hand in his. Maybe her freckles weren't quite as noticeable as she'd thought.

Las Vegas was at its best after dark. The casinos were enchanting with millions of lights illuminating their facades, each trying to outdo the other in brilliance and design.

"Do you mind if we walk?" Matt asked. "That way we don't have to worry about finding a parking spot every time we want to go into a casino."

"No." Traffic moved at a snail's pace to accommodate the pedestrians that filled the streets. Besides, walking would be fun.

They ate first in a casino that offered a dinner buffet of a hundred and fifty dishes. Then Matt cashed some money and handed Margaret a plastic tub of coins. "Try your luck."

"I have my own money," Margaret protested.

"You can use that later," Matt said. "This way if you win the million dollar jackpot, I'm entitled to half."

Margaret stared at him, glad to see the smile on his face, hear the teasing note in his voice. She had missed both lately.

They wandered in and out of casinos trying the slot machines and all the games of chance. In one casino, they watched a free circus act, in another they saw white tigers. Half an hour before midnight, Matt surprised her with tickets to a magic show, and when they came out of it, it was three in the morning.

"Sleepy?" Matt asked.

Margaret shook her head, looking at the picture a photographer had taken of them before the show. Matt had his arm around her shoulders, and she was laughing up at him. For once, Margaret thought, she looked almost pretty.

"What do you want to do next?" Matt asked.

Margaret was like a little child at the circus, and her pleasure made the night fun for Matt, too. In spite of her excitement she kept asking him what he wanted to do, and her consideration warmed him more than anything else.

Margaret intended to postpone the end for as long as she could. "I still have some money left. Do you mind if I try my luck at the slot machine once more?"

"I don't mind, Margaret."

At four o'clock, Matt looked at his watch and said, "We have to leave now. Come on."

She followed him outside, and Matt hailed a cab to take them back to the casino they were staying at. Margaret became conscious of the fact her feet and her back hurt.

To her surprise, instead of heading for their room, Matt headed for the parking lot. "Don't fall asleep on me now," he said as he opened the car door for her. "There's one more thing I want to show you."

Margaret watched in silence as he left the strip and drove north. She stared contentedly at the plastic tub of money in her hands. It didn't matter how much she was left with, the coins really represented the sum total of her happiness.

Matt had been the perfect companion. He played as diligently as he worked. Margaret knew he would give the same attention to loving. A shiver slipped down her spine as she thought of Matt's warm mouth, heating all it touched to molten lava.

"We're here."

Margaret stared out of the windshield as she caught a glimpse of water and a huge dam.

"Lake Mead," Matt announced as he pulled up in the marina. Opening the trunk of his car, he took out a navy blazer. In the gray light of dawn, they were the only people on the shore.

"You the bloke who called about the boat last night?" a voice asked grumpily. Margaret looked at the motorboat bobbing in the water, the man in it.

"I am." Matt handed the man a bill and said, "Sorry to get you up so early. We'll be back in a couple of hours."

The man looked at the money in his hand and hopped nimbly out of the boat. "Keep her for as long as you want, sir," he trilled, startling Margaret with his sudden change of mood.

She smiled. As usual, Matt knew the right buttons to punch to make everyone happy.

Matt placed the blazer around her shoulders and Margaret snuggled into it. She stood beside Matt as he guided the boat out into the middle of the lake.

"Where are we going?" she asked.

"You'll see," was all Matt said in reply.

She watched the sky as a band of pale pink erased the gray. Other hues appeared with each passing moment. Matt stopped the boat and wrapped both his arms around her. Margaret's pulses quickened as she leaned back in the cocoon of warmth.

The sun rose majestically on the horizon. The water took on soft opalescent hues, as it threw off the mantle of the night.

Margaret gave a small sigh of pleasure.

The sunrise, Matt's arms around her, the gentle lapping of the water against the boat, the sound of the birds greeting the new day, the taste of excitement in her throat, the scent of pine from Matt's blazer, all combined to fill her with contentment. Life had never been better.

Margaret knew it was because she had finally recognized one important fact. It was better to love someone than allow the fear of losing those one loved to rule her life. It didn't matter anymore that trucking was an integral part of Matt. It didn't matter that caring meant being vulnerable. She would rather have the love she felt now, come what may, than the emptiness she had lived with all these years. Margaret turned her face up to Matt.

"I love you, Matt," she said softly.

His arms tightened about her, and then she felt him drop a kiss on the top of her head. She turned toward him. He didn't say anything and some of Margaret's elation faded. She searched his face, and he put a hand up to cup her cheek. "We'll talk when we're not so tired, okay?"

That sounded reasonable. Only for once she didn't want reasonable. Margaret nodded, feeling suddenly close to tears. Instinct told her Matt had retreated from her because he didn't feel the way she did. Just because she had finally let go of her fears didn't automatically make him feel the same way.

The day was just as beautiful as it had been a minute ago, but for Margaret it was as flat as a bottle of wine left opened for too long. She watched quietly as Matt started the motor and turned the boat toward shore.

They drove back to Las Vegas in silence. At the door of her room Matt said, "Sweet dreams, Margaret. I'll come to you at nine-thirty."

Margaret woke up a couple of hours later feeling as good as new. Almost. Looking back, she tried to identify the source of the uneasiness that gnawed at her. Memories flooded into her mind. It had to do with Matt. She had told him she loved him. He hadn't said he loved her. It ought to have been perfect, but the moment had fallen short of the happiness mark. Her admission of love had in some strange way set them back instead of moving them forward.

Matt had admitted once that he had never trusted a woman on an emotional basis. Margaret swallowed. Had the fact she had told Matt she loved him this morning given him the impression that, like the women his father had married, she was impressed by their night on the town? Love could never exist without trust and unless Matt learned to trust he wouldn't be at peace with himself.

Matt dropped Margaret at the hospital on his way to the police station. A nurse informed Margaret her Timmy was fine. Dr. Patterson had examined him and declared there was nothing wrong that a little rest at home wouldn't cure.

"Would you like to sit with your brother while I find out what's happened to the discharge papers? Dr. Patterson was about to sign them when he was called to Emergency. I won't be long."

Margaret found Timmy watching a cartoon on television. She stood in the doorway watching his face, giving thanks that nothing had happened to him.

"Hi, sis!"

"Hi, Timmy. How are you feeling this morning?"

"I'm fine. The doctor says I only have to take the pain-killers he's described if I have a headache."

"Great."

Margaret slipped into the chair beside Timmy's bed, searching her head for a topic that wouldn't upset her brother.

"Summer's almost over," she said. "I'll be back in Washington soon."

"I'd like to go over part of the comprehension in the SAT manual with you before you return to Washington."

Margaret's startled gaze flew to her brother's. Had she heard right? "Of course."

"I'm sorry if I got you and Aunt Jan all worried yesterday." Timmy continued, "I really didn't mean to. I wasn't trying to take a risk or anything. It all happened so quickly I didn't know what was going on till I was lying flat on my back, looking at the sky."

"I know that."

"When I talked to Aunt Jan on the telephone yesterday, she started crying. It made me feel terrible. Then I saw your face when you came in and I guessed how worried you were, as well. I'm sorry."

He paused, and Margaret said quickly. "It could have happened to anybody."

Timmy looked at her, amazed. "You mean that?"

"Of course. Anyone could have come out of that rest area and apprehended the man. It just happened to be you."

"You mean you're not going to tell me this would never have happened if I hadn't gone on that run?"

"No."

Margaret knew she would never quite lose her tendency to worry about Timmy, but the smile on his face confirmed her first attempt at letting go had met with unqualified success.

"Mr. Magnum's downstairs, and I've got your papers," the nurse said, pushing in a wheelchair. "We're going to wheel you downstairs. Regulations."

Timmy opened his mouth to protest and then closed it, winking at Margaret. She smiled back at him, knowing that at long last things were really beginning to mend between her and Timmy.

Chapter Eleven

"What happened at the police station?" Timmy asked as soon as Matt steered the car out of the hospital parking lot.

Matt took his time answering and Margaret looked at him in surprise as he adjusted the rearview mirror and cleared his throat.

"I decided not to press charges against Mr. Frinton," he said at last, reluctantly.

"Why?" Timmy asked.

"When I talked to him he told me he's an ex-trucker. Last year after losing his wife and baby in an accident he turned up drunk at his job and was fired. His employers refused to listen to him, or consider taking him back. Stealing was Alec Frinton's way of getting back at the system. It was easy for him to study the habits of the drivers, jimmy the locks and remove a box here and there."

"Did he say why he picked *your* trucking company?" Margaret asked.

"No particular reason, except that many of my drivers always stop at that particular rest area, and generally there are very few other people around," Matt said. "Frinton said he took only enough to keep body and soul together... for him that meant being in a perpetual drunken stupor. He said he never meant to harm anybody...he just panicked when he saw you, Timmy."

"Why aren't you pressing charges?" Timmy asked.

"Everybody needs a second chance and I decided to give Alec Frinton one. I told him if he checked into an alcoholic rehabilitation center and remained there till he was cured, he could have a job in Bedouin Trucking."

"That was very generous of you," Margaret said, "but will the police agree to let him go?"

Matt nodded. "I convinced them Frinton has a better chance in the world as a recovered alcoholic than as someone with a criminal record. He's agreed to do community service as the law demands proper restitution, but since only my company was involved in the thefts and I refused to press charges they decided to let him go."

There was a small silence and then Matt asked, "Are you both upset that I didn't press charges?"

"No," Margaret said. "I think you did the right thing."

"I'm not mad," added Timmy. "Alec Frinton looked old and very scared. Besides, he got a bad rap from his trucking company didn't he?"

"He did, Tim."

Matt turned and looked at Margaret and she said, "Do you think Frinton will really check into a center?"

"I just dropped him off at one before I came to the hospital," Matt said. "The rest is up to him."

Matt was really good at getting other people to see things clearly and work out solutions for them, Margaret thought. Surely he could find a way through his own problems.

She couldn't tell him she was not like the other women he had known. For things to work between them he would have to arrive at that conclusion himself.

A little later Margaret glanced at Timmy, fast asleep in the back seat. The nurse on duty had warned her he might still be under the effect of the sedative he'd had last night.

"I've told Timmy to take the rest of the week off from work."

"Thanks, Matt." It would be easier coming from Matt than from her or Aunt Jan.

Her mind returned to the scene in the boat. Margaret swallowed. Talking, Margaret felt, wiped out the awkwardness of silence between them. "Vegas will be something to tell my friends at the Edwards Institute about."

"Are you looking forward to going back, Margaret?"

Margaret wasn't eager to leave Inchwater. Because of Matt. But Margaret had learned her lesson. Pride refused to let her say anything except a simple, "Yes."

He didn't say anything more, and after a while, lulled by the purring of the car and the soft music coming over the radio, Margaret fell asleep.

Visiting Gina the next afternoon, Margaret discovered things weren't getting any better for Jack and Gina, they were getting worse. Communication seemed to have broken down completely between them. Realizing nothing she said would help, Margaret listened quietly to Gina's tale of woe.

Thinking of the first day she had met Jack at Garrison Community Hospital, his obvious love for Gina, Margaret wondered why everything had changed so drastically. As she walked back to the restaurant Margaret tried to figure out what had gone wrong.

Was the stress of his job beginning to get to him? Margaret didn't blame trucking for Jack and Gina's problems, as she would have at one time. Every job had problems attached to it. It was a person's reactions to those problems that created personal stress.

In her room, Margaret looked at the pieces of the pattern she had cut out for a dress, wishing life came with patterns that could be followed to ensure perfect results.

The telephone rang a little later as she sewed the skirt of the dress, and Margaret picked up the extension in her bedroom.

"Margaret," Aunt Jan said. "Matt is on the other line for you."

Margaret's heart set up a wild drum beat. She hadn't really expected to hear from him so soon. Pushing a button, she said, "Hi, Matt!"

"Hello, Margaret!" His voice was like a warm embrace. Margaret felt the color rise in her face. The twenty-four hours since their return from Las Vegas had seemed empty without Matt.

"Trish called me a while back. She is having a Midsummer Night's Ball as a fund raiser for a diabetic hospital in Los Angeles. I was wondering if you would like to come down with me. It would give you an idea of how she works and you could tell Dr. Edwards about it." Matt's tone was friendly, nothing more, nothing less.

Margaret swallowed. Was this his way of letting her know that as far as he was concerned, nothing had changed between them?

"Margaret?" prompted Matt.

"I'll have to think about it," Margaret said quickly.

It would take time to think up a watertight excuse. She had never done anything like this before, had nothing to wear for such an occasion. What kind of conversation did one have with people who paid five-thousand dollars a plate for dinner? Besides, where would she stay in Los Angeles?

"When I mentioned bringing a guest, Trish said you were welcome to stay with her," Matt continued. "She has plenty of room and it won't be a problem."

"I'll think about it and call you back," Margaret said.

Later she wondered if Matt's invitation was some kind of a test. Did he want to see how she measured up in the society he had grown up in?

Matt, Margaret acknowledged, wasn't the kind of man to plan something like that. Even if nothing came of the way they felt about each other, Margaret had something to show Matt.

Pride insisted she had nothing to prove to him. Love said she did. Aunt Jan had told her Matt had mentioned once that the minute women discovered how rich his father was and saw the mansion in Malibu, they had stopped at nothing to gain Maximilian Magnum's attention. It was clear Matt thought all that mattered to women were a man's money and assets. To prove he was wrong, Margaret would have to accept the invitation and hope once she got to Malibu, she would find a way to prove to Matt all women were not the same.

Calling him at the truck stop before she could change her mind, Margaret told Matt she would be happy to attend the ball with him.

"I was wondering if you'd mind if we went down Friday morning," Matt said. "That way I can attend a business meeting Friday and we'll return Sunday morning."

"I don't want to impose on your sister," Margaret protested. "Maybe I could check into a nearby motel."

"It won't be an imposition," Matt said. "Trish's house is enormous, and there's an army of servants to go with it."

Margaret wondered if Matt was talking of the home he had grown up in. Wouldn't it hold painful memories for him to go back?

As if picking up her question telepathically, Matt said, "Trish and Susan wanted to keep the old house when my father died. The lower floor has been converted into administrative offices for PHP, People Helping People, the nonprofit organization they jointly run. The upper floor houses a cafeteria, two employee lounges and a conference room. Both my sisters have extensively remodelled former staff cottages on the grounds. They insisted on my having the old guest house, so you see, we really have plenty of space."

Running out of reasons not to stay with his sister, Margaret kept quiet.

"So it's settled?" Matt asked.

"Yes," Margaret said, a quiver of excitement running through her at the thought of the weekend ahead.

Margaret went downstairs to tell Aunt Jan about Matt's invitation.

Aunt Jan looked surprised, then pleased. "It will be a nice change for you, Margaret. And from what Matt has told me about them, his sisters sound really nice."

"What will I wear to the ball?" Margaret worried aloud. "I don't have time between now and Thursday to make something really special."

"You can go shopping once you get there."

Margaret's budget wouldn't really stretch to expensive. She tried to tell herself it didn't matter.

Oh yeah? Well, you may not admit it, but you want to hold your own in the midst of all the shimmer and glitter.

It was true. Margaret admitted she didn't want Matt to feel ashamed of her.

The mansion in Malibu was even more formidable than Margaret had imagined. The extensive lawns that surrounded the main house were punctuated by shrubs and plants that looked as if they bloomed to order.

"I'll just check if Trish is here." Matt pulled up in front of the main house and went inside. He had become increasingly silent for the last half hour. The silence was so unlike him that Margaret wondered what memories had returned to haunt him.

"She's at a meeting," Matt said, sliding behind the wheel of the car again. "We'll go to her place and she'll join us shortly."

He followed the wide drive lined with enormous California oaks and stopped in front of a house with a red roof and bougainvillea climbing up the sides. Margaret stared at it, enchanted with its picture-book prettiness.

A man opened the front door as they got out of the car. His face lit up at the sight of Matt. Matt shook the man's hand and put a hand on his shoulder. "How are you, Hook?"

Turning to Margaret, he said simply, "This is Hook, a friend of ours. Hook, meet Margaret Browning."

"Come in, please!" Hook said, throwing the door wide open. "I'll get your luggage later. I used to be Mr. Magnum's butler. Now, I look after Patricia. Matt has told me what good care your aunt takes of him in Inchwater. It's an honor to meet you."

She was ushered into a living room with a twenty-five-foot cathedral ceiling. Margaret looked around her silently. What was it Gina had said once? Looking at him, no one would guess how important Matt was. Gina had been right. Margaret for one, had never realized until today the wide chasm separating her world and Matt's. All he had told her; all she had surmised; nothing had prepared her for this aura of elegance and wealth that was an essential part of him.

No wonder he hadn't made any commitment. She fit in here as much as a dandelion would in those carefully manicured lawns outside. How could she have ever entertained the thought that they could be happy together?

Beside her Matt said, "Margaret, would you mind if I left you for a few minutes?"

Squelching the impulse to place a stranglehold around his neck and insist he take her with him, Margaret tried to smile instead. "Of course not."

"Hook will take good care of you."

Margaret stared blankly at the glass of lemonade Hook handed her, wishing she had insisted on staying at a motel.

"Did you have a good trip down from Inchwater, Miss?"

"Yes, thank you."

Where had she read that an experienced butler could size up the exact worth of a person and their clothing the minute he set eyes on them? Her princess look wouldn't help now.

"Won't you sit down?"

"I'd rather stand, thank you." She didn't want to crush the perfect cushions on the couch.

"Hello, there!"

Margaret turned as two women entered the living room.

"I'm Patricia," said the tall, slim one who looked as if she were taking a break from modelling, "and this is Susan."

"Sorry we weren't here to welcome you. The meeting went on longer than expected." Dressed in California casuals and designer jewelry, Susan looked like a petite Venus. In her sundress and light jacket, Margaret felt like apple pie next to French pastry.

Patricia smiled warmly. "Lunch will be ready soon. Let me show you to your room. I'm so glad you could come for the ball."

Margaret shook hands with both women, but, aside from a stilted, "How do you do," she could think of nothing to say except, "You have a beautiful home."

"Thank you," Patricia said. "It's too big for one person, but I love the space."

"You are having dinner with me tonight," Susan said. "I have to warn you, my house looks like it's on an earthquake fault, thanks to my three-year-old daughter. Pete and I are convinced we should have named her Calamity Jane instead of Melissa Ann."

Beneath their polished, immaculately turned-out exteriors, both sisters were warm and friendly. Just like Matt. Somehow it didn't do much to ease Margaret's tension. All around her were signs of wealth and breeding that went back several generations and separated her from them like a deep chasm.

Shown to an enormous bedroom, Margaret stared at her reflection in the mirror, and then leaned closer. Her hair seemed more orange then red today and five freckles seemed to have made their appearance since this morning. Margaret sighed. The three nights she was to spend here seemed to stretch ahead of her endlessly. No matter what she did, she would never fit in, let alone prove anything to Matt.

Margaret lifted her chin. She was going to get through this visit as best she could. In Inchwater, she would have plenty of time to grieve over her lost dreams of a future with Matt.

When Margaret rejoined Matt's sisters in the living room, Hook entered to announce lunch would be served in a few minutes.

"Where is Matt?" Susan asked.

"His car's not out front," Patricia said. "He must have some business to take care of."

"It's always business with him. I hope we're going to see a bit more of him than we usually do," Susan grumbled.

The sound of the doorbell made her face brighten, and she turned toward the door as Matt walked in, holding a smiling little girl by the hand.

This had to be Melissa Ann, Margaret thought, as Susan hurled herself into her brother's arms for a hug and a kiss, to be followed by Patricia. There was no doubting the affection the trio shared. With an arm around each of them, Matt smiled at his sisters and Margaret swallowed the lump in her throat.

"Mommy, I'm here too," Melissa Ann said.

"So I see," Susan said, picked up her daughter and gave her a kiss. "Who invited you?"

"Uncle Matt told Mrs. Dolby I could come to lunch," Melissa Ann announced importantly. "He said it would be more fun with me here."

As their gazes met, Margaret wondered if Matt had guessed her earlier tension. It *was* easier with Melissa Ann around. The child was an icebreaker and kept the conversation rolling with her questions.

"I'm caught up with arrangements for the gala for the rest of the day," Patricia said over lunch. "But please make yourselves at home and ask Hook for anything you need. He will take you wherever you want to go. He knows the best places for sightseeing, shopping and eating."

"All I have to do is get a dress for the ball," Margaret said.

The sisters exchanged a look, and then Patricia said quickly, "It's going to be a masked ball and we're all going to wear costumes from Shakespeare's period."

There was a moment's silence before Matt said with a frown, "Why didn't you mention this earlier?"

Susan looked guilty. "Trish and I thought you might not show up for it if we told you, Matt. You know how fussy you are about dressing up."

The sisters exchanged another quick look and then Susan turned to Margaret. "Haggerty's in downtown L.A. has the best costumes for rent. Patricia and I picked out a few extra costumes when we got ours, and asked Poco

Haggerty, the owner of the store, to hold them for us. Hook will take you there after lunch.''

"Can I wear a costume, too?" Melissa Ann asked anxiously.

"Yes," Susan said. "After your nap, you can put on your fairy costume.''

"I'm a good fairy," the little girl informed them. "When Daddy comes home, I'm going to change him into a frog. Then, when Mommy kisses him, he's going to change back into a prince. My mommy likes kissing my daddy.''

Everyone laughed, while Susan blushed.

"Margaret, do you like kissing Uncle Matt?" Melissa Ann asked, looking directly at her.

Margaret's face flamed, while three adults sprang into action around the table.

"Come see the new fish in the pond, Melissa Ann" Hook said, who was removing their plates.

"I'll get dessert." Patricia was on her feet, and out of the room.

"It's time for your nap," Susan said in a firm tone. *"Now."*

Melissa Ann's chin wobbled for a minute before she turned to her uncle quickly and said, "Uncle Matt, will you read to me before I take my nap?"

"Of course," Matt replied.

"And can I ride on your shoulders all the way home?"

"Yes." Matt stood up and reached for his niece. "Let's go, now." Looking at Margaret, he said, "Excuse me. I'll see you tonight at Susan's.''

"I'm sorry," Susan apologized as she made to follow her brother and her daughter. "I never know what she's going to say next.''

"Don't worry. I'm used to children," Margaret assured her.

After lunch, Hook drove her to Haggerty's. Margaret looked around in awe. Hundreds of costumes lined the walls of a large showroom. Hook came in with her and handed Patricia's card to the girl at the front desk.

"Please sit down," the receptionist said, rising quickly when she saw the name on the card. "Mr. Haggerty has been expecting you."

A few minutes later Haggerty came out to meet them. Margaret had a hard time not letting her mouth fall open as she took in the ponytail, the false eyelashes and the powder on the man's face.

"Miss Browning. Charmed." He extended a hand for her to shake. "Come into my private salon, please. Any friend of Trish and Susan's is a friend of mine."

Margaret followed him, feeling like Alice in Wonderland.

"These are the four costumes Trish asked me to keep for you," Haggerty said as they were brought in by an assistant. "After you make your selection, we can pick out the accessories."

Margaret looked at the rich, heavy dresses with their enormous skirts and matching wigs and made no move to touch them. She couldn't see herself in any of them and she wasn't about to wear one simply to fit in with the crowd. Thinking of the theme of the ball gave her an idea.

Haggerty turned to Margaret, one penciled eyebrow raised. "And which would you like to try on first, madam?"

"I've decided to make my own costume," Margaret said quickly. "These are too elaborate for me."

Haggerty looked insulted. It was apparent she had slipped several hundred notches in his estimation.

"I see," he said with a sniff. "If you'll excuse me..."

He floated away, and Margaret made her way to the door.

"You didn't find anything you liked, miss?" Hook asked, opening the car door for her when she walked out of the store.

"I've decided to make my own costume. Do you know if there's a fabric store nearby?"

She expected condescension from him as well, but Hook's expression didn't change. "There's one four blocks from here. Unless I'm mistaken, there's a sewing machine in storage that might help you."

"Is there?" Margaret said. Though the design she had in mind was very simple and she had a day and a half to make her dress, a machine would simplify her task. "If it's not too much trouble to get it out, I'd like the use of it."

"No trouble at all, Miss."

Encouraged by Hook's manner, Margaret said, "Have you been with the Magnums a long time?"

"Ever since Matthew was born, miss. I watched him grow up. Life wasn't easy for him or the others then and I don't think it is easy for them now to bury that part of their lives. They all have a great capacity for giving love. Believing they can receive it in return is very hard for them. The Colonel almost lost Susan by giving up too soon."

Margaret wondered if this was Hook's way of telling her if she loved Matt she would need patience and tenacity.

They stopped at a fabric store, and Margaret selected material and sewing aids. Back at Trish's house, Margaret shut herself in her room and spread the fabric on the bed. Cutting without a pattern, she would have to be very careful not to ruin the heap of gauzy material.

Margaret wondered where Matt was. She could imagine him holding his niece, her curly head resting against his chest as he read to her. She had seen the warmth in his eyes as he looked at his sisters, but his manner to her had definitely changed. Convincing him of anything was not going to be easy.

Chapter Twelve

Patricia returned at four. As they sat on the deck sipping iced tea, she asked Margaret about the Edwards Institute. Talking about her work and the children, Margaret found herself relaxing.

"Dr. Edwards called me a week ago to thank me for the offer to help raise money," Patricia informed her. "He said he doesn't want me to plan anything yet unless he knows for sure if there is someone who will run a second institute as he wants it run. He sounded very serious. The kind of people I usually work with want to know how much I can raise for them and how soon."

Margaret thought of the quiet, gentle doctor whose work was his whole life. "The children come first with Dr. Edwards," Margaret told Patricia, "and he won't settle for anything but the best for them."

Patricia's question revealed a genuine interest in the institute, and Margaret told her about the children and the work Dr. Edwards did with them.

They left for Susan's place at six. Margaret found it easy to relax with Melissa Ann showing her all her toys, and Pete, Susan's husband, talking about life in the army. There was nothing in anyone's manner to make her uncomfortable, but Margaret was nervous. Matt and his sisters stood leaning against the deck rail chatting, and she wondered what he would think of the dress she was making for the ball.

Matt loved the way Margaret's face lit up as she smiled over something Pete said. He looked away to find both his sisters watching him.

"You love her, don't you?" Susan quietly said. It was more statement than question.

"Yes."

"It shows when you look at her," Trish added.

They saw Pete move toward the barbecue and Susan said, "I'm going to show Margaret the house and garden while Pete gets the barbecue going."

Matt couldn't fathom the look his sisters exchanged. He and Trish watched Susan, Margaret and Melissa Ann go into the house.

"Are you going to marry Margaret?"

"What?" Matt said.

Trish didn't flinch at his tone. "I know you're the big brother, but can I tell you something?"

"Go ahead," Matt said resignedly.

"Our father didn't only leave us his money. He left each of us with recollections of a past that cannot be erased."

"Yes." Denying a fact never altered it.

"Whenever you found yourself attracted to someone, you back off. I do the same. Marriage scares us because we think of it as a battlefield that leaves indelible scars."

"Isn't it?" Matt asked dryly.

Trish shook her head. "Susan has proved you get out of marriage what you put into it. Dad's life-style isn't a measuring stick for our own lives. Nothing can change the old memories, so it's best to leave them buried, build a new life over them."

"It's easier said then done," Matt said.

"We have to shed the burden of the past, Matt. Every human being needs to be loved because it is the only emotion that signifies total acceptance of another. My therapist explained Dad's behavior as the constant search for someone who would love him for himself. She said we *have* to believe someone can love us for ourselves before any relationship can work. Without that faith we don't stand a chance."

"How long have you been seeing a therapist?" Matt asked.

"Since I lost the man I loved."

Matt turned to look at his sister. He hadn't known about a love affair gone awry. "When did this happen?" he asked.

Trish shrugged. "Around the time you moved to Inchwater."

He could pinpoint the time now. Returning after a two-month stay in Inchwater, he had commented on how much weight Trish had lost. She had told him it was the new fashion. During that visit, she had seemed busier than ever.

Trish sat down next to him. "Therapy helped me see quite a few things clearly. All three of us share the same vulnerability, the need to be accepted. It's one reason all three of us are so involved in charity work, but that's no substitute for a permanent, warm, loving relationship with the right person."

Matt said nothing and, after a while, Trish said, "Susan and I want you to know one more thing."

"What is it?"

"Three months ago, I met Alice Huntley. Do you remember her?"

"Yes." She had been their father's third wife. Or was it his fourth?

"Strange as it may seem, Alice and I have become friends. We have lunch together once a month. She told me she left Dad because he was always trying to control everything she did. Whom she met, where she shopped, little things that shouldn't have mattered. Though outwardly he put on a big show of being the perfect husband, according to Alice, he was obsessed with having complete control of everything and everyone in his life. She said all the fur coats and diamonds in the world weren't worth being manipulated as if she were a windup toy."

Matt frowned. "Are you saying Dad *drove* the women in his life away?"

Trish nodded. "Yes, just like he drove us away."

Matt thought about what Trish had told him as he helped his brother-in-law with the steaks. It was too much to sort out all at once.

After dinner, Matt turned to Margaret and said, "Let's go for a walk."

Margaret threw a startled glance around the redwood deck. They couldn't possibly leave the minute the meal was over. Patricia was discussing costumes with her brother-in-law. Susan could be heard telling Melissa Ann she had fifteen minutes left before bedtime.

"The others won't miss us." Matt stood up and said, "I'm going to show Margaret around. Thanks for the dinner, Sue and Pete."

Margaret echoed his thanks, feeling awkward.

From the side of Susan's house a path sloped down to the beach. Halfway down on a promontory was a gazebo with wooden seats around the sides. In the center a heap of cushions rested on the floor.

"Shall we sit here?" As Margaret sat on a cushion, Matt sat on the wooden step of the gazebo.

Margaret stared at the ocean. The scents of night and the chirping of insects surrounded them. If she turned her head, she could make out the lights of Los Angeles. "What a beautiful spot," she said.

"It is, isn't it?"

Taken aback by the harsh note in his voice, Margaret kept quiet. She had noticed the tension about him when she had complimented Susan on her home earlier. What was wrong with appreciating something beautiful?

As Margaret looked at the waves glistening in the moonlight below, the pain she had sworn not to give in to surged up in her. Matt must be comparing her to the women his father had known, thinking she was as impressed by the Magnum estate as they had once been.

Anger was a hot flame inside her as she said, "It was a mistake to bring me here, Matt."

"What do you mean?" Matt ran a hand through his hair. The gesture reminded her of Timmy, and convinced her Matt was deeply upset.

"I feel like a fish taken out of my nice, safe bowl and tossed into the ocean. Being here has proved to me we don't have anything in common. I know now what that last missing link keeping us apart is. It's the difference in our backgrounds."

"It is not," Matt ground out. "It's the thought I might let you down, that I might not have what it takes to sustain a marriage. That you'll grow bored and leave me."

"You're keeping your memories alive by feeding them with your fears," Margaret said angrily. "You think every woman is like the ones your father knew, that no woman can love you for yourself. Are you going to let what happened to your father control the rest of your life?"

Matt stared at her. "What do you mean?"

"You've got answers for everyone's problems, why don't you take a good look at your own?" Margaret demanded. "Susan and Patricia share the same memories you have, but I don't see them dwelling on them the way you do."

Margaret swallowed. It was too late to stop now. "You told me once, we each place ourselves in personal cages, that Bedouin freed you from yours. He did to a certain extent, but not completely. Only you can free yourself, Matt."

He didn't say anything and Margaret stared out at the water through the tears that filled her eyes. "No matter how much you have in the way of money and assets, Matt, you'll always be poor unless you can open yourself up to love. I hope someday you will get over your fear and trust someone enough to share your life with them."

Leaving the gazebo, Margaret climbed the path leading back to the house. She heard Matt behind her but didn't turn around. If she said anything more now, she wouldn't be able to regain control. Matt followed her to Patricia's door, opened it for her, and then left without a word.

Margaret went to her room, thankful Patricia was still at Susan's. She didn't want to face anyone now. She felt as if she had just lost something that mattered a great deal to her. She was glad she had said what she had, though. Matt had to face his past. Only he could open the door of his personal cage and set himself free.

Matt stared at the rising tide from where he sat on the rock. It swirled in like the eager flow of his bitter thoughts carrying him back into the past. Picking up a stone, he flung it as far as he could into the water. Like his efforts to break free of his memories, it was immediately lost.

Margaret was right.

He had to let go, but he wasn't sure he knew how. Every time he returned to the house, memories smothered him. Some of his were like the ones Margaret had of her parents. They could be taken out and shaken, to free them of dust that clung to them. Others were so deeply ingrained in the very fabric of his being that Matt didn't know how to get rid of them. There was no viewpoint that would alter them.

Matt picked up another stone, hurled it away from him. He thought of everything Trish had told him, searching his heart and soul for answers. It was a while before he rose and climbed up the hillside to his lonely house.

Late the next evening, Matt rang the doorbell of Trish's house. He ran a finger along his collar to ease the stiffness. The crimson cloak of his costume billowed out behind him, and the crown on his head was awry. Melissa Ann had told him he looked like Snow White's father, which did nothing to appease his mood. He looked and felt silly. Dressing up was for kids.

Patricia opened the door and the smile on her face slipped a bit as she saw the crackle of irritation on his face.

"Come in. The others are all here."

The sight of Pete, uneasy in his page boy outfit, helped to ease Matt's mood a bit. At least he wasn't going to suffer in solitude. Exchanging a sympathetic smile with his brother-in-law, Matt looked at his sisters. Susan was going as a tavern wench, Patricia as Portia, the young lawyer who had fought for her husband's innocence.

"Where's Margaret?" Matt asked.

She had been on his mind all day. He'd wanted to call her from work but he hadn't, because what he had to say had to be said in person. He had to apologize for the way he had been lately and discuss his fears with her before he lost her. The thought he had hurt Margaret disturbed him deeply and Matt had found it impossible to concentrate on work. At an afternoon meeting, he had been called upon three times before he had been able to answer a question.

"Margaret will be here soon," Patricia said. "She's making a last minute adjustment to her costume. Wait till you see it."

"It's absolutely gorgeous," added Susan.

They heard the sound of a door opening and Margaret's footsteps. She paused in the doorway of the living room, and her gaze flew to his.

Matt stared. She wore a dress that floated dreamily about her in some soft material. Knotted at her shoulders, the dress hung straight to the floor, the points of the fringed hem barely sweeping the floor. Her shoes seemed to be covered with the same material as her dress.

The wonderful green color reminded Matt of shiny new leaves in spring. As she moved he glimpsed the silky sheath she wore under the green chiffon. Her hair, unbound and fiery red, hung down her back. On her head rested a wreath of crimson berries nestling amid dark green leaves. Her mouth returned his smile, but the distant look in her eyes didn't change.

"Titania, Queen of the Fairies," Susan announced. "Margaret is going to be the belle of the ball."

"You look absolutely wonderful," Patricia added.

Matt followed them silently out to the limousine that was to take them to the ball. There was something different about Margaret tonight. A confidence he had never seen before was evident in the tilt of her head, in the way she moved. She looked like a red-haired witch about to cast a spell on everyone she met.

Margaret felt a wonderful satisfaction as she stepped into the limousine. The dazed look in Matt's eyes as he'd looked at her had made all the trouble she'd taken with her costume worthwhile. She wasn't going to fight him on the decision he had made about marriage, but she was going to correct the impression he had of women.

Margaret watched the crowd swirl and separate as a live band supplied music. She sat with Pete, Susan and another couple at a table on the edge of the dance floor, noticing the costumes and the elaborate hairdo's that went with them.

Margaret searched the dancers for a tall figure in a crimson cloak. She had shared the first dance with Matt, not really sure why he had asked her to dance. Other than hold her close, he hadn't talked to her at all. Matt probably felt it was a token gesture his sisters would expect of him. Convention satisfied, he had disappeared.

Patricia had introduced her to a stream of people and mentioned that Margaret taught seriously handicapped children. To Margaret's surprise, quite a few people were interested in learning more about the Edwards Institute. Margaret had patiently answered all their questions. She danced with a film producer, a musician and a man who told her he could buy the Empire State Building if it was for sale. She had received compliments on her dress, her face, her figure and two invitations to leave the party with men she had barely talked to for five minutes. Margaret had finally escaped from all the new faces, saying her feet hurt. She felt like the ice sculpture of the child gracing the center of the buffet. Lost, melting, *superfluous*.

She was surprised to hear Susan say, "Whenever we come to these occasions we tell ourselves never again, but it's hard on Trish if we're not here to support her. As it is, she does most of the work. As for Matt, it's nothing short of a miracle that he's here today."

The remark surprised Margaret. She had thought Matt would take occasions like this in his stride.

"He hates what he calls the emptiness of it all. He says people come just to show off their latest clothes and jewelry, pull everyone they know to pieces and then go home discontented because someone had on something more expensive than them."

Matt approached the table a little later. "Would you like to dance?" he asked Margaret.

She shook her head quickly. She wasn't going to be his *duty*. "My feet hurt in these new shoes."

"Mind if I sit with you?"

"Of course not."

Margaret told herself not to waste time wondering why Matt chose to sit with her when he could be dancing with one of the stream of gorgeous women present. She turned away to reply to something Pete said, trying to focus on what he was saying. Matt's closeness had her heart beating so loudly she could barely hear Pete.

Matt had watched Margaret dance with some of the guests, seen the polite mask she had donned with them, the keep-your-distance look. She may have been impressed by the house in Malibu, but she wasn't impressed by any of the people here tonight. He had seen her excuse herself from a group when one of the men, a young producer, had started boasting about how much money he had spent on his last motion picture. Her dignity had affected him as nothing else could when another man had placed an arm around her shoulders. Politely but firmly she had moved away from his side. If she was bored, or felt out of place, she didn't show it.

Matt looked around and decided he'd had enough. Bending, he whispered in Margaret's ear, "Would you like to leave now?"

Margaret turned to him in surprise, "Won't Patricia think it odd if we slip away?"

"She'll understand."

When the limousine pulled up in front of Trish's place, Matt turned to Margaret. "Margaret, we have to talk."

Margaret looked at Matt and shook her head. "Not now, Matt. I'm very tired." Her voice was sad but firm.

The evening had been more of a strain than she had imagined. She felt like a runner completing a marathon, who realizes there is nothing left to train for. Empty, drained, *bereft*.

Whether or not she had proved anything to Matt was immaterial. Nothing could bridge the gap between his world and hers.

She didn't want to talk to Matt in this mood because, if she did, desperation might make her beg him to hold her and make love with her. Right now, she didn't care if it was just for one night ... at least she would have that to remember.

He hesitated a moment and then said, "Good night, Margaret."

"Night Matt."

It wasn't going to be a *good* night, simply a rerun of the last few where her mind spun around searching for answers and came up blank.

The two-and-a-half hour return drive to Inchwater the next morning was strangely quiet. Matt seemed preoccupied with his thoughts and Margaret considered how best she could get on with her life. Nothing she had done or said had made a difference to Matt and she had to admit defeat. The sooner she got used to the fact there was no future for them together, the better.

The trip to Yosemite turned out pleasant but uneventful. Margaret walked among the redwoods every day, missing Matt more than ever, going over and over in her mind everything that had happened since she had first met him.

Though she had decided to resign herself to the fact Matt didn't love her, a part of her refused to give up. The happy, refreshed look on Aunt Jan's face made Margaret feel the vacation was worthwhile, but she wanted to be back in Inchwater with Matt.

The four-hour return drive in the car Margaret had rented for their vacation seemed to take forever. When they pulled up in front of the restaurant, Margaret took the key out of the ignition and turned to Aunt Jan. "I'll be back in a little while. I want to see Mikki and Gina."

It would help pass the time. Margaret planned to stop by the truck stop later, when there weren't so many people around to talk to Matt.

"Aren't you tired?" asked Aunt Jan, surprised.

Margaret shook her head, "Not really. I'll be home soon."

Gina loved the silk scarf Margaret had brought her back. She kept touching the soft fabric and saying, "It's beautiful. I'll always treasure it."

Margaret, busy noticing the changes in her goddaughter, said, "I'm glad you like it. How's Jack?"

Gina looked much happier. "Everything's fine between us again. Janet insisted on Jack telling her what was wrong. Jack said becoming a father had made him feel he should provide his daughter with the best of everything, that's why he was working the long hours. Janet told him it was important for Jack to discuss how he felt with me."

"And . . ." prompted Margaret.

"I mentioned what Jack said to Dr. Reddy and he said it wasn't uncommon for a first-time parent to feel that way. He talked to Jack and me and explained that while some new fathers reacted like Jack did, others simply disappeared because they couldn't handle the responsibility. He said we should talk to each other often and see a counsellor if we needed any more help."

"And . . . ?" Margaret prompted again.

"It took a bit of talking to convince Jack that Mikki won't care if she is dressed in designer clothes or not. It's more important for her to have her father around while she's growing up. We've made out a budget, and if it doesn't work, I'll work part-time at the restaurant."

Relieved at the way things had turned out, Margaret said, "There isn't really any happily-ever-after, is there? It's just the way a couple deal with the situations around them that makes a difference to the quality of life."

"That, and remembering to keep the romance alive," Gina said. "Janet reminded Jack it doesn't cost a thing to say, 'I love you,' and yet some people never think to say those words."

Recalling her argument with Matt in the garden, Margaret smiled. That must be something all men needed to learn.

Taking Mikki from Margaret, Gina placed the baby on a brightly colored exercise mat on the floor. "Will you have dinner with us tonight? Now that Jack is on the Los Angeles run, he's back by five every evening. Since Matt left we haven't had anyone over, except Timmy. That boy looks so happy these days."

"Matt has left?" Margaret couldn't hide the dismay in her voice.

Gina turned from the stove. "Men! Didn't he tell you he was leaving?"

The slow burn of anger inside Margaret fanned itself into a flame. So, this was what tough men like Matthew Magnum did when the going got tough? They ran away. It was very easy for him to sort out everyone else's problems, while his own remained in cold storage forever. Well, he wasn't going to get away with that.

"What time does Jack leave for L.A. in the mornings?" Margaret asked. She didn't know when the decision to go after Matt, tell him how she felt, had materialized. She just knew it was there now, and she had to do something about it. She had been mistaken to think nothing could bridge the gap between Matt's world and hers. Love would bridge any gap if it was given a chance.

"Seven," Gina said. "Why?"

"Tell him I'm going with him tomorrow. I can't stay now, Gina. I have a few things to do at home."

Like plan how I'm going to tell Matthew Magnum off, Margaret thought, slapping an oatmeal pack on her face a few minutes later.

And she was going to look absolutely beautiful doing it, too. Breaking four eggs into a bowl, she added vinegar to the mixture, and then began to massage the sticky concoction through her hair. With her hair wrapped up in a turban, Margaret pulled everything out of her closet. Old-fashioned, was she? Not so old-fashioned to take his decision lying down. She would show him.

Timmy came to the door a while later, took one look at the clothes piled on the bed and quietly went to his room. He didn't think Margaret would want to go into Garrison and watch a movie with him tonight. She had something on her mind.

Jack followed Gina's gaze to the figure that approached. In a white suit and high heels, Margaret looked like she had just stepped off the cover of the magazine his wife loved reading.

"God help the man. Margaret's got her war paint on."

Something about the immense satisfaction in his wife's voice made Jack look at Gina closely. "Anything going on that I should know about? I don't want to get into any trouble with Mr. Magnum."

Gina reached up and planted a smacking kiss on her husband's mouth. "Don't worry. You aren't the man trouble is headed for," she reassured him with a chuckle. "Just make sure Margaret gets to L.A. in one piece."

Nodding, Jack turned away to climb into the truck. He heard Gina say something to Margaret with a laugh. All the talk about war paint made Jack nervous. A man had no defence against a determined woman, and Mr. Magnum had been very nice to him. Was he letting a hornet's nest loose around the boss's head by agreeing to take Margaret to L.A.?

Jack stared at Margaret as she got into the truck. He had never seen her look more beautiful, or more distant.

Grabbing a towel, he wiped the passenger seat as he said, "Good morning, Margaret."

"How are you, Jack?" Margaret asked sweetly from under the brim of her hat. "Will you please drop me off at Mr. Magnum's headquarters in L.A.? I have some unfinished business to settle with him."

Jack nodded, "Yes, ma'am."

Jack had told Matt about the advice he had gotten from Janet. He just hoped Matt remembered it. *I love you,* were three little words that could make a big difference.

Gina stood with Mikki in her arms, waving them off, a huge smile on her face.

Margaret turned to Jack. Now that they were actually on their way, she felt some of her courage slip. Chasing after Matt did not seem such a good idea at all. She twisted the shoulder strap of her bag.

Jack may not have been married all that long, but he could tell when Margaret's mood switched from confident to nervous. Leaning forward, he switched on the CB radio. A little conversation might distract her.

Margaret listened to the voice over the air until she heard a familiar one. "This is Lone Wolf, heading for Los Angeles. Anyone know if it's still there?"

"Lone Wolf, this is Waltzing Matilda. I'm heading for L.A., too. What do you mean, is it still there, mate?" A voice with an unmistakable Australian twang asked.

"Well, Waltzing Matilda, you know everyone's expecting the big earthquake to hit L.A. any day," Lone Wolf replied. "Asking if it's still there is just my little joke."

Jack picked up the CB handpiece. "Lone Wolf, this is Proud Papa. I was in L.A. yesterday. It's still there."

"Proud papa, how's your baby doing?" Lone Wolf asked.

"Great," Jack said. "As a matter of fact, I have Mikki's godmother with me today."

Jack gave her the handpiece. Margaret swallowed. "This is Rose Red. Good morning, everybody."

"Rose Red, this is Lone Wolf. Did you find the cove all right the other day?"

"We did, thank you. It's a beautiful spot, Lone Wolf."

The memory of Matt leaning over her, of her own response, made Margaret's pulses quicken.

"Where's that man of yours? What was his call name, now? Bedouin Two?"

"He's in Los Angeles," Margaret said.

"Ah, going to visit him, are you?" Lone Wolf asked.

Margaret swallowed. "Not exactly."

"Rose Red, this is Waltzing Matilda. Did you just mention Bedouin Two?"

"Yes," said Margaret.

"Well, I picked up his call sign a little while ago. He was talking to another driver named Grizzly Bear."

Margaret stared at Jack. Where was Matt heading?

Jack took the handpiece from her and said, "Waltzing Matilda, this is Proud Papa. Are you sure?"

"Sure as there's hair on my chest," came the quick reply.

He was going away on one of those long trips he liked taking. Margaret realized she wouldn't be able to talk to him after all. Unless she did so right now. Margaret turned to Jack. "Jack, do you think we might be able to reach him on the CB?"

"I'll try," Jack said. "Bedouin Two, are you out there? Come in Bedouin Two. This is Proud Papa."

Jack repeated the call at five minute intervals. On his third try, the CB crackled in response. "Proud Papa, come in. This is Bedouin Two."

Jack handed Margaret the handpiece. Taking it from him she said quickly, "Matt, this is Margaret."

There was a few moments of absolute silence, and then Matt said, "Margaret, what are you doing in Jack's rig?"

"I was coming to Los Angeles to see you."

"Why, Margaret?"

Margaret swallowed and looked at the handpiece in dismay. Since yesterday, she had imagined so many different scenes with Matt. In his office, in his car, in his home. None had included talking to him over the CB in this manner.

"Margaret, are you there?" Matt asked.

"I'm here, Matt. I had to see you. There's something I have to say to you in person."

"What is it, Margaret?"

His voice was fading. Panicked, Margaret wondered if he was getting out of range. Out of her life. Quickly she said, "Matt, will you marry me?"

Beside her, Jack jumped. There was pin-drop silence on the air, and Margaret felt her cheeks burn as Matt didn't answer. If there was one thing worse than making a fool of oneself in private, it was doing so in public. What had Matt said about the CB? That there could be as many as a hundred people listening in to a frequency at one time?

"Maybell calling Star Gazer. Star Gazer, are you listening in?" A woman's voice cut into the air.

"Maybell, this is Lone Wolf. If you value that perfumed hide of yours, you'll stay off the air. The lady is in the middle of a proposal."

There was a second's silence again, and then Maybell said, "A proposal? She isn't proposing to you, is she Lone Wolf? Now, that *would* be a reason to cut in. Save one of my kind from a fate worse than death." A shrill laugh followed the statement.

"Enough," Waltzing Matilda yelled. "Anyone speak out of turn, and they'll have to reckon with me at the next truck stop. Go ahead, Rose Red."

Margaret swallowed hard and said, "Matt, listen to me. It doesn't matter if you choose to drive a truck or move to

Beverly Hills. I just want to spend the rest of my life with you, no matter what."

"What more could a man ask for?" Waltzing Matilda asked aloud.

"Shut up, Waltzing Matilda," Maybell said. "If you don't stick to your own rules, *you'll* have to answer to *me* at the next stop."

"Yeah, keep out of this," Lone Wolf said. "Anyone can see, they need privacy."

Jack jerked a thumb out of the window. Margaret looked out of hers and swallowed hard. There was a line of trucks behind them, and in the next lane, staying as close together as they could. Privacy was impossible. Everyone apparently wanted a ringside seat for the show.

"Margaret, where did you think I was going?" Matt asked.

"I thought you were headed off on one of your long trips," Margaret said.

"I am on my way back to you, Margaret. To make another attempt to get you to listen to me."

"You are? Why did you leave in the first place?"

"Yeah, why did you, mate?" Waltzing Matilda chimed in.

Matt ignored Waltzing Matilda's comment. "Margaret, I know marriage doesn't come with any warranty, that all it does is give a couple a base to build the rest of their lives on. I was going to tell you the night of the ball that I loved and trusted you, that I'd been all kinds of a fool, but you wouldn't talk to me. Then later, I thought maybe you had changed your mind about me. I realized you didn't like some of the people you met, and I thought you might have decided you didn't want anything to do with me. But as soon as I was in L.A., I realized I would be the biggest fool if I let you go without making it clear how I felt about you. If you'll have me, I'll do my best to make all your dreams come true. I love you."

Margaret blinked to hold the sudden tears back as a loud cheer came over the CB.

"Way to go, mate!"

"Rose Red, he's a good man," Lone Wolf said.

"This is all so romantic," sniffed Maybell.

"Jack, the next rest area is half a mile away," Matt instructed. "Pull up there. I'm right behind you. Ever since I've known Margaret, she's shown a very poor sense of timing."

"Anyone else stop there beside the two love birds and I'll knock their blocks off," Waltzing Matilda threatened. "Congratulations, you two."

Other listeners chimed in with good wishes as Jack drew into the rest area. A long line of trucks pulled past, tooting their horns and waving as Margaret got out of the truck. Five minutes later, Matt drove up.

He jumped down from the cab of his rig and Margaret flew into his arms. Many long, satisfying kisses later she said, "I can't believe I just proposed to you over the air."

Matt cradled her in his arms and smiled. "I can't believe you did that, either, my old-fashioned love." His eyes darkened as he said, "I'm sorry I put you through so much while I sorted myself out, but I knew you deserved better than a man who couldn't free himself of the past."

Margaret covered Matt's mouth with her hand. "No apologies. Your honesty and the way you always shared your innermost thoughts is what made me fall in love with you. Our pasts are part of us and as long as they don't interfere with the present, they don't matter."

Matt rested his forehead against hers. "I've always loved you, Margaret, always."

"Oh," Margaret said, "but at Lake Mead—"

"I was an absolute fool," cut in Matt. "I was searching for some sort of guarantee, dwelling too much on my father's experiences. Trish made me see my memories were best buried, that for years I'd had the wrong impression of things. Being with you convinced me that I had to let go of the past and concentrate on us, Margaret.''

"I'm glad, but even if it returns to haunt you, I want to help you deal with it," Margaret said.

"I'll never shut you out again, Margaret." Matt picked up her right hand and kissed each finger and then her palm. "Where would you like to go on our honeymoon?" Matt asked as he pressed kisses down the side of her neck. "Europe? The Orient? Australia?"

Margaret cupped Matt's face and brought his mouth back to hers. It was a while before she could think about her answer. "None of those places will do," she said softly. "I want a trucking honeymoon."

"What?" Matt drew back to look at her.

"You heard me," Margaret said. Her expression held a combination of shyness and love. "I want you all to myself. No people around, no interruptions, a bed close by."

A glint came into Matt's eyes. "If I hadn't promised Janet the pleasure of arranging your wedding, we could have gone straight to Vegas and been man and wife by tonight."

"Aunt Jan was in on this, too? Don't worry, she'll arrange things quickly, you'll see," Margaret said. "Besides, I want to have the people who matter to us, at our wedding—Tim, your sisters, Pete, Melissa Ann, Joe, Jack, Gina and a whole heap of other folk."

"Susan and Trish will help your aunt. You realize that the guest list now includes every trucker who will be close to Inchwater on that day?"

Recalling the avalanche of gifts dropped off for Mikki, Margaret said, "They can all come, but no presents. Instead, anyone who wants to make a donation to the new Edwards Institute is welcome to do so."

"Have you thought about where you want to live?" Matt asked.

"Wherever you are," Margaret said. "But I'll have to return to Washington till Dr. Edwards can hire a substitute. I can't let him down."

"Of course not," Matt said. "We can rent an apartment there and I can commute, when needed, to L.A. and Inchwater. Eventually, I'd like to make Inchwater our base," Matt said. "It's a great place for kids to grow up in." He drew back and searched her face. "Of course, that's a decision we'll have to make together."

"What is?" asked Margaret absently, fitting her finger into the cleft in Matt's chin.

"Kids," Matt said hesitantly. "Do you want any?"

Margaret drew back in the circle of his arms to look up at him. "Of course. I can't promise I'll be the most exemplary woman in the labor ward, but I can't imagine life without children."

Matt hauled her to his chest and looked down at her, a glint in his eye. "Kids are a long way down the turnpike. Right now the sooner we get back to Inchwater, the sooner Janet can arrange the wedding."

Margaret nodded. "Let's go home and tell everybody our news—if they haven't already heard it from another trucker. They'll all pitch in to help Aunt Jan."

The road of life stretched ahead. Margaret knew there would be ups as well as downs, but with Matt at her side she wasn't afraid anymore. She smiled up at him as he urged her toward the cab of his truck. She was in just as much of a hurry to begin married life with her tender trucker as he was.

* * * * *

HE'S MORE THAN A MAN, HE'S ONE OF OUR

Fabulous Fathers

Dear Christina,

Stationed here in the Gulf, as part of the peacekeeping effort, I've learned that family and children are the most important things about life. I need a woman who wants a family as much as I do....

Love, Joe

Dear Joe,

How can I tell you this...?

Love, Christina

Silhouette
R O M A N C E ™

=== HEARTLAND ===
HOLIDAYS

Christmas bells turn into wedding bells for the Gallagher siblings in Stella Bagwell's *Heartland Holidays* trilogy.

THEIR FIRST THANKSGIVING (#903) in November
Olivia Westcott had once rejected Sam Gallagher's proposal—and in his stubborn pride, he'd refused to hear her reasons why. Now Olivia is back...and it is about time Sam Gallagher listened!

THE BEST CHRISTMAS EVER (#909) in December
Soldier Nick Gallagher had come home to be the best man at his brother's wedding—not to be a groom! But when he met single mother Allison Lee, he knew he'd found his bride.

NEW YEAR'S BABY (#915) in January
Kathleen Gallagher had given up on love and marriage until she came to the rescue of neighbor Ross Douglas ... and the newborn baby he'd found on his doorstep!

Come celebrate the holidays with Silhouette Romance!

TAKE A WALK ON THE DARK SIDE OF LOVE

October is the shivery season, when chill winds blow and shadows walk the night. Come along with us into a haunting world where love and danger go hand in hand, where passions will thrill you and dangers will chill you. Come with us to

In this newest short story collection from Silhouette Books, three of your favorite authors tell tales just perfect for a spooky autumn night. Let Anne Stuart introduce you to "The Monster in the Closet," Helen R. Myers bewitch you with "Seawitch," and Heather Graham Pozzessere entice you with "Wilde Imaginings."

Silhouette Shadows™
Haunting a store near you this October.

**It's Opening Night in October—
and you're invited!
Take a look at romance with a
brand-new twist, as the stars
of tomorrow make their
debut today!
It's LOVE:
an age-old story—
now, with
*WORLD PREMIERE
APPEARANCES* by:**

Patricia Thayer—Silhouette Romance #895
JUST MAGGIE—Meet the Texas rancher who wins this pretty
teacher's heart...and lose your own heart, too!

Anne Marie Winston—Silhouette Desire #742
BEST KEPT SECRETS—Join old lovers reunited and see what
secret wonders have been hiding...beneath the flames!

Sierra Rydell—Silhouette Special Edition #772
ON MIDDLE GROUND—Drift toward Twilight, Alaska, with this
widowed mother and collide—heart first—into body heat
enough to melt the frozen tundra!

Kate Carlton—Silhouette Intimate Moments #454
KIDNAPPED!—Dare to look on as a timid wallflower blos-
soms and falls in fearless love—with her gruff, mysterious
kidnapper!

**Don't miss the classics of tomorrow—
premiering today—only from**

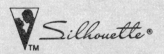

PREM

Take 4 bestselling love stories FREE

Plus get a FREE surprise gift!

Special Limited-time Offer

Mail to Silhouette Reader Service™

In the U.S.	In Canada
3010 Walden Avenue	P.O. Box 609
P.O. Box 1867	Fort Erie, Ontario
Buffalo, N.Y. 14269-1867	L2A 5X3

YES! Please send me 4 free Silhouette Romance™ novels and my free surprise gift. Then send me 6 brand-new novels every month, which I will receive months before they appear in bookstores. Bill me at the low price of $2.25* each—a savings of 44¢ apiece off the cover prices. There are no shipping, handling or other hidden costs. I understand that accepting the books and gift places me under no obligation ever to buy any books. I can always return a shipment and cancel at any time. Even if I never buy another book from Silhouette, the 4 free books and the surprise gift are mine to keep forever.

*Offer slightly different in Canada—$2.25 per book plus 69¢ per shipment for delivery. Canadian residents add applicable federal and provincial sales tax. Sales tax applicable in N.Y.

215 BPA ADL9   315 BPA ADMN

Name	(PLEASE PRINT)	
Address		Apt. No.
City	State/Prov.	Zip/Postal Code.

This offer is limited to one order per household and not valid to present Silhouette Romance™ subscribers. Terms and prices are subject to change.

SROM-92   © 1990 Harlequin Enterprises Limited

Silhouette
R O M A N C E™

★ WRITTEN IN THE STARS ★

WHEN A SCORPIO MAN MEETS A CANCER WOMAN

Luke Manning's broken heart was finally healed, and he vowed never to risk it again. So when this Scorpio man introduced himself to his neighbor, Emily Cornell, he had companionship on his mind—plain and simple. But just one look at the lovely single mom had Luke's pulse racing! Find out where friendship can lead in Kasey Michaels's PRENUPTIAL AGREEMENT, coming this November only from Silhouette Romance. It's WRITTEN IN THE STARS.